LOSING
THE ICE

BY

JENNIFER COMEAUX

Losing the Ice
by Jennifer Comeaux

32103574

*To Christy Bloom for being an awesome plotting buddy
and freeing me from my writer's block!*

Chapter One

November, 2010

I loved my boyfriend.

I loved Josh's sweetness, his sensitivity, his passion, and his creativity. I loved how respectfully he treated me both as his girlfriend and his skating partner, and I loved how his clear blue eyes could melt me all over with just one look.

But his family...

They made me want to run screaming into the hills.

Or the Cascade Mountains as was appropriate at the moment.

We were in Portland, Oregon for Skate America, our first competition of the season, and I had mere minutes to prepare for the arrival of Josh's mom and sister from Los Angeles. To thicken my skin for the criticisms and cold stares I knew would come.

"Courtney, can I get a smile?"

I snapped back to reality and realized the photographer was talking to me. I loosened my tense face into a semblance of a smile as the event volunteer snapped the photo for my credential badge.

I moved to the adjacent booth to wait for my badge while Josh stepped in front of the camera. We'd been dating a year, and I still found myself completely mesmerized by him. His dark hair and blue eyes were a killer combination, but it was his shy smile that stood out the most. It always added an extra beat to my heart.

The volunteer manning the booth handed me my credential, and I snorted at the photo. The drizzly Portland weather had wreaked havoc on my long, curly hair, so my photo was nothing but a small pale face surrounded by a large poof of blond frizz.

"I look like the Cowardly Lion." I showed Josh the picture as he joined me.

He laughed and squeezed his arm around me. "You look adorable."

"I think you're a little biased."

He accepted his badge and placed it next to mine. "Our first credentials as a team. We'll have to frame these."

A different kind of tension crept into my shoulders — the nervous kind. Josh and I had been scheduled to compete in Japan in October, but Josh's injured knee had forced our withdrawal. We'd both endured injuries over the summer that had stolen training time and prevented us from doing any early-season competitions.

Josh and I had competed the past ten years with different partners and had just teamed up eight months ago after our partners retired. There was a lot of buzz surrounding our partnership, but with all the ice time we'd lost, I was feeling less than confident about our debut.

"Earth to Court." Josh waved his hand in front of my dazed eyes.

"Sorry." I rattled my head. "Lots on the brain."

"My family?"

"That's one big thing." I looped the credential lanyard around my neck. "I'm still not sure why they're coming when they've never been supportive of our partnership or our relationship. They've barely spoken to you since February."

"Maybe they're ready to make peace."

"Or they could be coming here hoping we'll fail so they can gloat," I said as we exited the hotel ballroom.

"Let's not think the worst."

It was hard not to when all I'd ever received from Josh's family was coldness. His parents had expected him to go to law school and work at his dad's firm in Beverly Hills, but Josh had scrapped those plans when he'd asked me to skate with him. Mama and Papa Tucker saw me as the evil temptress who'd caused Josh to "throw away his future." Never mind that he'd had no desire to be a lawyer in the first place.

We entered the lobby and were greeted with hugs from fellow members of Team USA who'd just arrived. A loud crash made me jump, and I looked to the other end of the room. Something made of glass had shattered all over the tile floor, and the three women sitting next to the crash site were a mixture of amused and horrified. Appearing at that moment in the doorway and looking anything but amused were Josh's mom and sister, Stephanie. My stomach tightened as I hoped the smashed glass wasn't an omen of a disastrous weekend ahead with Josh's family.

Stephanie and Mrs. Tucker detoured around the mess in their heeled boots, and they marched to the front desk, not noticing Josh and me. My first instinct was to run away before we could be seen, but I'd only be delaying the uncomfortableness. And if I truly wanted us to all get along, I couldn't hide from them.

Josh laced his fingers through mine and warmly pressed our palms together. I gave him a nod, and we started forward.

Stephanie saw us first, and she swooped her arms around Josh before he could say anything. He gave me a wide-eyed look over her shoulder. The only time I'd seen her show him that much affection was when they'd made the Olympic team.

"Hey, Steph," Josh said.

She remained quiet, and when she stepped back and turned to me, all her affection was gone. I received the same pursed lips and I-think-I'm-better-than-you look she'd always given me.

"How was your flight?" I attempted small talk.

She removed her white cashmere hat and fluffed her long brown hair. "It was a flight."

Mrs. Tucker finished at the desk and pecked Josh's cheek, kissing more of the air than his face. "It's good to see you, Darling."

She hadn't seen her son in almost a year and that was the most she could muster? I would never understand that woman *at all*.

"I'm glad you could come," Josh said. "Is Dad going to make it?"

"No, he had some meetings he couldn't reschedule."

She still hadn't acknowledged me, not even with a cursory glance. Josh reunited our hands and slid closer to my side, reminding me again why I loved him so much. I squeezed his fingers tightly and looked directly at Mrs. Tucker. She couldn't ignore me now.

"Thank you for coming to support us," I said. "It really means a lot to us."

Mrs. Tucker's narrowed blue eyes shifted in my direction but then quickly refocused on Josh. "I hope you haven't eaten dinner yet. I'd like you to join us."

"We haven't. What time should we meet you?"

Mrs. Tucker flashed another quick look at me. "I'd prefer just family tonight."

Josh's whole body clenched. "I'm not going without Court."

"It's just dinner," Stephanie said.

"It's more than that." Josh's voice grew harder. "It's the

fact that you need to accept Courtney because she's going to be part of this family one day."

Whenever he mentioned our future I got all gooey inside, but the idea of Bethany Tucker as my children's grandmother ruined some of my warm fuzzies.

"Fine," Mrs. Tucker relented. "We'll meet you here in an hour."

An hour? I groaned to myself. I was hoping to get the torture over with as soon as possible. Josh's mom and sister rolled their designer luggage past us, and he and I moved away from the bustle at the front desk.

"What were you saying about not thinking the worst?" I asked.

He let out a long breath. "Maybe dinner will be a good chance for us all to talk and come to an understanding."

"I don't think one dinner is going to change her mind about me. Especially with Stephanie egging her on with rude comments."

"I warned Steph to lay off last time I talked to her. I don't expect her to be Miss Sunshine, but she can be civil."

I rubbed my neck. "I can literally feel the tension taking over my muscles."

"Thank you for putting up with all this." Josh kissed the top of my head.

I looked up at him and touched his cheek. "There's nothing I wouldn't do for you."

He gazed at me a few moments before he wrapped me in an embrace and spoke low in my ear, "I know how I can relieve your tension."

My spine tingled, and I pulled back to see Josh's eyes shining at me.

"When does your roommate get in?" I asked.

"Tomorrow." His gaze flickered down to my mouth, sending another electric current through me.

An hour until dinner sounded *sensational* now.

I grabbed both Josh's hands, and we didn't waste a minute getting to the elevator.

****

I was still floating from my Josh-induced high when he and I returned to the lobby an hour later, but Mrs. Tucker's steely glare quickly grounded me. She slipped her phone into her humungous purse and tightened the belt on her black trench coat.

"I made a reservation at Ruth's Chris," she said. "The concierge said it's on the next block."

"That's a steakhouse," Stephanie complained.

"They serve salads," Mrs. Tucker said as she pushed open the glass door.

I shook my head. She obviously gave no consideration to her daughter's vegan diet.

The spitting rain had stopped, but the evening air still held a wet chill. Josh hugged me to his side as we walked the short distance to the restaurant. My phone buzzed in my purse while the hostess sat us at a table (after Mrs. Tucker refused a booth), and I typed a quick response to Mom's text.

"Important message?" Mrs. Tucker sniped.

A sharp reply shot onto my tongue, but I clamped my lips shut. *Don't be sassy. Be the better person.*

"It was from my mom. She and my dad are arriving tomorrow, and she wanted to double check our practice time."

Mrs. Tucker lifted one perfectly sculpted eyebrow. "I didn't think they'd be able to make the trip."

"Why not?"

"Well, it's a long way from Boston. Flights must be expensive."

Ah, her usual dig about my family's financial status.

"They can afford a lot more now that they don't have my skating expenses."

"That's right. You and Josh have your own private benefactor." Her mouth pressed into a thin line. "What was her name? Mrs. Connor?"

"Mrs. Cassar," Josh said.

"She's actually flying in with my parents," I said.

I couldn't wait for Mrs. Cassar to meet Josh's mom because she wasn't one to hold her tongue. The elderly widow was a regular at the Cape Cod restaurant where Josh and I worked, and she'd been our cheerleader since before we'd even teamed up. It was only because of her generosity in covering our skating expenses that we were able to compete together.

After we finished ordering drinks and food, my phone dinged again, but I left it alone. Mrs. Tucker was watching me closely over the rim of her martini glass. I thought she might make another comment about my parents, but she turned to Josh instead.

"Are you still playing piano at that restaurant?"

The way she said *that restaurant* made it sound like a truck stop.

Josh nodded as he sipped his water. "I play Thursday, Friday, and Saturday nights now. And I'm teaching piano in the afternoons."

"I thought you were going to do choreography," Stephanie said. "You're so good at that."

"I'm doing that, too. I worked with a couple of skaters at our rink and also up in Boston."

"Takes a lot to pay the bills, doesn't it?" Mrs. Tucker said pointedly.

When Josh's parents had cut him off financially after we'd paired up, they'd seemed to think he wouldn't survive on his own. But I'd never doubted he'd do just fine.

"I'm busy, but I'm loving everything I'm doing," he said.

Mrs. Tucker hummed quietly in response. "What about you, Courtney? You're still bartending?"

"Yes... I am."

"And you've continued to live with your coaches." The snide tone of her comment couldn't be missed.

I sat up straighter and cleared my throat. "I've never taken advantage of Emily and Sergei's generosity. I've offered to pay them rent, but they won't let me, so I help out with the twins and any other way I can."

"I'm surprised you haven't shacked up with Josh yet," Stephanie said.

Josh sent her a warning glare while I took a long gulp of water. This was exactly how I'd expected the dinner to go, but it didn't make it any easier to sit through.

"He lives in that woman Mrs. Cassar's pool house," Mrs. Tucker said. "I'm sure Courtney would rather stay at Emily and Sergei's spacious home."

I set my glass down with a hard thump. "If Josh and I wanted to live together, I'd be happy in a cardboard box with him."

So much for not being sassy.

"Only because you know he has a trust fund to fall back on," Mrs. Tucker sassed in return.

I gritted my teeth and held in my comeback. She was baiting me into an outburst. She wanted nothing more than for me to act like the classless girl she thought I was.

Everyone stayed silent, deeply breathing in the tension, until Josh said quietly, "Why did you come?"

Mrs. Tucker tilted her head slightly. "Why did I come?"

"You obviously haven't accepted the choices I've made or changed your attitude toward Court."

"I came to see what you gave up your guaranteed successful future for."

A decent mother would've said, *I came to spend time with my son who I haven't seen in months.* But no. That wasn't her motivation.

"So, you're not here to support us," Josh said. "Do you

even want us to skate well?"

"What I want is for you to be successful in life, and doing odd jobs and skating with your girlfriend isn't going to get you there."

I let out a loud, frustrated breath. "It's not like he's flipping burgers... not that there would be anything wrong with that... but you heard him before. He loves the work he's doing, and he gets to use his amazing talent every day."

Josh folded his napkin and calmly placed it on the table. "We're not staying for dinner. I'm not putting Court through another hour of this."

He stood, and I glanced at Mrs. Tucker's and Stephanie's stunned faces before getting to my feet.

"You already ordered your meal," Mrs. Tucker said.

"Tell the waiter he can take it home," Josh said as he helped me with my jacket.

"You don't have to leave. We can talk about something else." Stephanie shot a sideways dagger at her mother.

Josh shrugged on his own jacket. "I'm sorry, but I don't see any hope for this conversation."

He put his hand on my lower back, and I took his cue. Neither of us looked back, and we didn't speak until we reached the stoplight at the crosswalk.

"I don't know why I thought that would go any differently," Josh said.

"Because you have an optimistic heart." I caressed the back of his neck.

We crossed the slick street and kept going past the hotel. I had the feeling Josh needed to walk out his frustration.

"I want us to kill it this weekend to show her how wrong she is." He picked up his pace, and I quickened my step. "Not that she'd ever admit it."

"I think she'd rather wear discount clothes for a week than do that."

He didn't appear to catch my attempt at humor as his

forehead creased with intense thought. "If we skate great, she might not admit she's wrong, but she'll know it."

What if we don't skate great? I wanted to ask but couldn't bring myself to say out loud. I hadn't told Josh how nervous I was because I didn't know if that would make *him* more anxious. Since we hadn't experienced a competition together yet, I hadn't learned how he dealt with the pressure.

Nothing like figuring out those important things at a major international event. With our biggest critic in the front row.

Chapter Two

I patted my stockinged thighs and rubbed them hard to stay warm. The backstage area of the Rose Garden Arena felt colder than the walk-in freezer at work. I couldn't wait to get moving in our short program so I could defrost.

Josh sat beside me, staring down at his folded hands. He wasn't a loud person by any means, but this was quiet even for him. He hadn't said much of anything during our six-minute warm-up on the ice or the entire time we'd been backstage. I'd been holding in a nervous bundle of chatter all evening. If he needed silence to stay in his competitive zone, then I would give it to him. First lesson I was learning about my new partner.

Em picked up our water bottles and offered them to Josh and me. "Need a drink?"

"I'm good, thanks," I said, while Josh looked up and silently shook his head.

Em had made the trip alone with us since Sergei had to accompany their novice and junior teams to Eastern Sectionals in Pennsylvania. I adored both my coaches, but Em and I had an extra-special relationship, so I was glad she was there for the start of this new chapter of my career.

"Time to get ready." She motioned us toward the corridor to the ice.

I unzipped my Team USA jacket, and when we reached the end of the hallway I gave it to Em. My hands fidgeted with the braids woven into my up-do, then the halter neckline of my rose-colored dress, and then the hem of my short skirt. Josh stepped in front of me, and he gently grasped my shoulders, stilling me. I stared up at him and took in a slow breath.

His long-sleeved, V-neck shirt showed off his lean muscles and matched the color of my dress perfectly. We'd worn our costumes at a dress rehearsal at home, but looking at us together now, standing just a few feet from competition ice, it really hit me.

We are a team. We are truly a TEAM.

The jitters shaking my legs kicked into a higher gear, and if Josh hadn't been holding onto me, I probably would've collapsed into a trembling heap. He rubbed my arms with long, warm strokes, and slowly my butterflies simmered down.

His eyes roamed over me and met mine with a deep gaze. "God, you are so beautiful."

My butterflies fluttered their wings happily, and I locked Josh in a tight hug. Leave it to him to be practically mute all night and then to say something so sweet.

"I just want you to know..." His soft voice tickled my ear. "Skating here with you tonight is an absolute dream come true for me."

I pulled back and framed his face with my hands. "I am *so* happy to be doing this with you."

He smiled. "Then let's do it."

We walked out under the bright lights of the arena and joined in the applause for the Canadian team taking their bows. As soon as they approached the boards, I pulled off my skate guards and hopped onto the ice. While I glided around the rink, loosening my legs, I slowly stretched my arms over my head and out wide. It was a relaxation technique Josh had shared with me.

He skated to my side, and we slowed to a stop in front of Em at the boards. She focused her bright blue eyes on us and patted our hands.

"I know you've waited for this a long time, so just enjoy every moment. Feed off the incredible connection you have with each other."

We nodded and each took a quick sip of water before we turned away from the boards to receive our introduction.

"Our next team represents the United States. Ladies and gentlemen, please welcome Courtney Carlton and Joshua Tucker."

My heartbeat thumped in time with the loud applause from the crowd. I looked at Josh, and he gave me a wide smile. I could see the excitement brimming in his eyes. We skated to center ice and spent the next few seconds and a few deep breaths getting into our starting position. My right hand rested on Josh's chest while his cupped my hip. Our eyes met and didn't let go.

The romantic piano notes of "Kissing You" began, and we started slowly across the ice, still locked in our gaze. Goosebumps lined my neck and my arms, and I let myself bask in the magic of the moment for just a second. Then I quickly thought about our first element, the explosive triple twist.

Josh took my hand, and we moved side by side, building up speed with only a few strokes. I envisioned my body spinning in the perfect twist right before I stabbed my toe pick into the ice. Josh tossed me up above his head, and I curled into three tight revolutions. When I came down safely in his strong grip, I exhaled and kept my eyes on Josh's as we flew around the corner of the rink.

The warmth of Josh's hand left mine as we split apart for our side-by-side triple Salchows. My body tensed with anxiety, and I repeated over and over to myself, *Free and easy. Free and easy.*

I pushed off with my back inside edge and spun three times in the air. My right blade landed on the ice with a scratchy thud, but I held firm for a clean exit. I couldn't see if Josh had completed three rotations, too, but he smiled at me, and I suddenly felt a lot looser. *He must have done the jump cleanly, too!*

Reining in my excitement, I focused my energy on the next tricky element, the throw triple flip. The music climbed higher, and Josh sprang me into the air right on the crescendo. I spun so fast I almost wasn't ready for the landing when my blade hit the ice. Once again I kept my leg steady and rode out the deep curve, and I got an even bigger smile from Josh.

We stroked forward and sped into the step sequence, which took us from one end of the rink to the other. Josh and Em had choreographed it together, and every step accented the nuances of the beautiful song. We twizzled in perfect unison to finish the sequence, and Josh took my hand once more to prepare for our overhead lift.

The people in the stands whooshed by me as we powered forward. Josh swung me up above his head with a lasso motion, and he began to rotate, not losing any speed. I started to change positions, but I felt Josh's feet losing their grip on the ice. Panic seized my chest, and I fumbled to grasp Josh's shoulder for support.

No, no, no.

Josh reached up and grabbed me as his skates flew out from under him, and we crashed to the ice, my body on top of his. The back of his head slammed onto the hard surface, and I gasped in terror as his eyes shut.

"Josh?" I slid off him, and the cold stung my legs. "Josh!"

I touched his cheek, but he didn't move.

"Josh!"

I leaned over him, hoping to see his eyes open, flutter, *anything*. But there was nothing.

Oh my God.

"Help!" I yelled toward the ice door, but the rinkside paramedics were already shuffling over to us.

The music had stopped, and everything was so quiet. One of the medics gently pulled me away from Josh's lifeless body while the others swarmed around him.

"Are you okay?" She looked me over.

All I could manage was a dazed nod. Josh had cushioned my fall. He'd taken the full brunt of it. And now he wasn't waking up.

Oh my God, oh my God.

My throat burned with tears, and I covered my mouth with both hands. The medics had Josh surrounded, so I couldn't see what they were doing to him. The lady holding my shoulders tried to coax me to leave the ice, but I wouldn't budge.

"I'm not leaving him." I shook my head violently.

"Court!" Em called from the open ice door.

She looked like she wanted to run out to me, but she couldn't in her heels. She waved for me to go over to her, and when I refused, she motioned more forcefully. I finally gave in but kept watching the medics as I skated away from them. They had strapped a brace around Josh's head and were putting him on a stretcher.

Em swept me into her arms the moment I reached her. "You're okay?"

The fear in her voice made me cry even harder. I nodded and pressed my face to her wool dress.

"He hit his head so hard," I said between sobs.

She hugged me tighter. "He's going to be okay."

I wanted to believe that, but I couldn't shake the image of

Josh falling unconscious right before me. Watching his beautiful blue eyes go dark to the world.

The medics were carefully taking Josh off the ice, and I started to rush forward to meet them. Em held me back and said, "I'll ride with him to the hospital. You get changed, and we'll get you there as soon as possible."

"I have to go with him!" I cried.

Our federation team leader Marni took charge of ushering me backstage. "One of the volunteers will drive us. We'll only be a few minutes behind the ambulance."

"I'll call Josh's mom to let her know where we're headed," Em said.

She gave me one last intense hug before hurrying after the paramedics. I raced to the locker room and did the quickest change of my life. Normally I took meticulous care of my skates, but I just threw them in my bag. When I came out to meet Marni, my parents and Mrs. Cassar were standing with her.

Mom embraced me first and Dad followed. I soaked in all the comfort from them I could, but nothing could ease the fear in my heart.

Mrs. Cassar grasped my arms firmly. "Joshua is a strong young man. You remember that."

The way she called Josh by his full name always made me smile, but hearing it then only made me tearier. As we all hurried outside, Mom and Dad gave me more assurances and I just kept nodding. They had to be right. Josh *had* to be okay.

Thankfully, the ride to the hospital wasn't long because my nerves couldn't handle another second in the car, not knowing what was happening. We found the emergency room, and Josh's family was already there with Em. Stephanie spotted me, and her puffy, red eyes narrowed. She stalked toward me and stopped inches from my face.

"This is your fault!"

Chapter Three

The anguish pressing on my chest made taking a breath difficult. But I forced a deep one and leveled my eyes with Stephanie's.

"Get out of my face."

She didn't listen and instead stepped closer. "Josh and I were partners for ten years, and he was never hurt like this. You've been his partner for ten minutes, and he ends up in the hospital!"

"Stop." Em took Stephanie's elbow. "It was an accident."

Stephanie shook her off. "They shouldn't be skating together. I said all along it was a horrible idea. And now Josh is lying in there…"

Her voice caught, and she pivoted and stalked over to her mother. Mrs. Tucker looked up from the paperwork she was completing as Stephanie sniffled loudly. My dad slipped his arm around me, but I stood tall because Mrs. Tucker was headed toward me. Unlike Stephanie, she showed no sign of tears. Only the same icy demeanor she always had.

"If you hadn't caused Josh to change all his plans, we wouldn't be here right now," she said. "So you *are* to blame for this."

Dad stiffened. "Now, listen—"

"So, you're Joshua's mother." Mrs. Cassar came forward, her pointy chin tilted upward. "You're exactly what I expected."

Mrs. Tucker folded her arms. "And you must be Mrs. Cassar."

"Yes, I am. We would've met before now if you cared enough about your son to visit him."

"Excuse me?"

I wiped my watery eyes to see Mrs. Tucker's indignation clearly. I'd expected Mrs. Cassar to have some words for Josh's mom upon meeting her, but I had a feeling the stressful situation was going to make those words even harsher.

"Joshua is one of the finest young men I've ever known. He would make any mother proud." Mrs. Cassar's eyes blazed as bright as her dyed-red hair. "Except his own, apparently."

"I want what's best for Josh."

"What's best for him is being with this wonderful young lady and skating with her." Mrs. Cassar gripped my arm. "If you really gave a damn about him, you would see that."

Mrs. Tucker's expression darkened further, and Em quickly inserted herself between the two women. "Why don't we all focus on good thoughts for Josh right now? That's what's most important."

"Yes, it is." Mrs. Cassar said. "Not blaming innocent people."

"There is nothing *innocent* about this girl." Mrs. Tucker shot me another dirty look.

The tornado of emotion churning inside me could no longer be contained, and my hands flew to my head. "Oh my God! Josh could be seriously hurt, and you're more worried about insulting me."

"Because we wouldn't be here if it wasn't for you!" Stephanie cried.

"Please keep your voices down," the nurse behind the desk warned.

I spun and retreated to the opposite side of the waiting area — as far away from Josh's family as I could get. Em followed me and drew me into her arms. I clung to her petite frame, and she held me quietly until I pulled back to look at her.

"Was there any sign of him waking up in the ambulance?" I asked.

"The medics were around him, so I couldn't see everything that was happening."

"What if... what if he doesn't..."

I tried to swallow the hard lump in my throat, but it strangled me. I couldn't stop the fresh round of tears from flooding my cheeks.

"He will." Em said confidently as she clutched my shoulders. "He will."

We hugged again and sat in the chairs along the wall, holding hands and remaining silent. I was too busy praying, *Please, please, please let Josh be okay.*

After what felt like hours, a white-haired doctor emerged through the huge double doors, and he huddled momentarily with Mrs. Tucker and Stephanie. They started toward the exam rooms, and I chased after them.

"Is Josh awake? I'm coming with you."

"You are *not* family." Mrs. Tucker held up her hand as a stop sign.

"I'm more his family than you've ever been."

She was about to respond when Em came to my side and pleaded, "Let her go in. Please."

I didn't wait for consent. I charged past the Tuckers and walked directly behind the doctor. He led us down a wide hallway and stopped at a room with a half-open door. My heart crashed against my chest in anticipation of what I'd find inside.

I walked into the room and sucked in a breath. Josh was lying on the bed in a hospital gown.

And his eyes were open.

A cry of relief escaped my lips, and I flew to the bed. I was so overcome I couldn't speak, so I put my hand on Josh's cheek to let him feel my love for him.

He turned his head slightly and winced, but he quickly covered it with a little smile. "Hey, don't cry. I'm okay."

"Okay?" I squeaked. "You were unconscious."

Behind me I heard the doctor tell Mrs. Tucker that Josh needed a precautionary CT scan to make sure he didn't have more than a concussion.

"See?" Josh covered my hand with his. "Just a little bump on the head."

His voice sounded groggy, and his eyes showed pain with every tiny movement he made. He might be trying to downplay his injury, but I'd heard how hard his head had slammed onto the ice. I'd never forget that awful sound.

"Can I see my brother, please?" Stephanie nudged my arm.

I didn't appreciate her trying to shove me out the way, but I wasn't going to have an argument with Josh lying there in obvious pain. I started to back away, but Josh held onto me.

"Stay here," he said.

I smiled and squeezed his fingers. Stephanie scowled, but the lines creasing her forehead showed she was more worried than annoyed.

"Do you know how scary it was watching you fall like that?" she said.

"I'm sorry you had to see that," Josh said.

A nurse came in and took the doctor aside to speak to him, so Mrs. Tucker moved to the foot of the bed. She looked back and forth between Josh and me.

"I hope this will be the end of this ridiculous partnership," she said.

Josh gave her an unblinking stare. "I'm not quitting."

"What if you hit your head again? Are you aware of the dangers of multiple concussions? Do you want to ruin your future even more than you already have?"

I gaped at her. *Really?* This was the conversation she wanted to have five minutes after finding out Josh wasn't seriously injured? Where was the joy, the thankfulness he was awake and talking to us?

"Your father can speak to the dean at UCLA," she continued. "I'm sure he can reopen your admission."

"I said I'm not quitting," Josh spoke louder and grimaced.

I was about to go off on his mom when an orderly appeared with a wheelchair, and the doctor said it was time for the scan. I bent and placed a gentle kiss on Josh's lips, and he tugged on my hand again as I tried to leave.

"I'm sorry we didn't get to finish the program," he said.

I shook my head. "Don't even worry about that."

"It was two of the best minutes of my life. I can't wait to do it again." He glanced around the room. "With a different ending."

I smiled and gave him another kiss, and he finally let my fingers slip from his. After the orderly wheeled him down the hall, I quickly returned to the waiting area to give everyone the good news. We exchanged hugs all around, and Mrs. Cassar said, "I told you Joshua would be fine. Nothing was going to keep him from you."

Mrs. Tucker was still giving me the evil eye, so we camped out on the far end of the waiting room until the doctor arrived with the results of the scan. When he said everything looked good, I placed my hand over my heart and sent up a silent prayer of thanks. Josh had to stay overnight, but it was just an extra measure of precaution.

"Do you want to try to see him before we leave?" Em asked me. "It'll probably be hours before he's moved to a room."

"Oh, I'm not leaving."

"You'll have to sit in the waiting room all night," Mom said. "Come back to the hotel and get some rest."

"I'm staying, too," Stephanie declared.

I gave her a curious look, and Mrs. Tucker said, "Josh will be sleeping. There's no need for anyone to stay."

"There might not be a need, but I *want* to be here," I said.

"So do I," Stephanie said.

Since when did she start copying me — the girl she hates?

Em watched us both warily. "Maybe I should stay, too, then."

I couldn't help but smile. "You don't have to babysit us. We'll play nice. Won't we, Stephanie?"

"I'm not here to talk to you. I'm here for Josh."

I sighed. I preferred to be in peace and not have Stephanie's bitchy vibes around, but I couldn't fault her concern for her brother.

Josh's room was going to be on the sixth floor, so Stephanie and I took the elevator upstairs. Our ride was silent and so was the deserted waiting room. I parked myself in the corner chair where I could stretch out and recline against the wall, while Stephanie took a seat on the other end of the long row of chairs. She removed her leather boots and curled her legs under her, and she tapped her manicured nails on her phone with rapid-fire speed.

I took out my own phone and pulled up the Facebook page Josh and I had created when we'd teamed up. Countless fans had posted messages wishing Josh well and saying how sorry they were about the accident. A few people we'd met at practice in Portland had posted photos of us beaming at each other as we'd run through our programs. My eyes misted as I gazed at our huge, excited smiles. We'd never thought our first performance together would end so disastrously.

I shook off the pity party and dabbed my eyes. Josh was

going to be fine. Once he healed, we could pick up where we'd left off before the fall — skating just like we'd dreamed of doing.

My battery was creeping lower, so I put away the phone and watched Stephanie stare at the TV hanging from the low ceiling. Her eyes weren't really focused on the *Friends* rerun, though. She appeared lost in thought.

I had often wondered if Stephanie had been born without a heart… if there was actually a hollow space in her chest like the Tin Man. But her excitement at seeing Josh upon arriving in Portland coupled with her emotional reaction to Josh's injury made me think she may actually be somewhat human.

"You miss Josh," I said.

She spun her head to face me. "Excuse me?"

"It must be hard not having him around. You guys were together for so much of your lives."

"Are you a psychologist now even though you've never taken one college class?"

I leaned my head against the wall and deeply inhaled and exhaled. "I was trying to have a pleasant conversation for once. It's just nice to see how important Josh is to you."

"Of course he's important," she snapped. "He's my brother."

She might continue to be hostile, but I wasn't going to stop trying to wear her down. She and I didn't have many chances to speak alone, and this might be my one opportunity to change our frigid dynamic. There was zero likelihood I would ever break the ice with Mrs. Tucker, and Mr. Tucker was usually MIA, so Stephanie was my best shot at making any alliances in that family.

"I think you're the only one in your family who really appreciates Josh's talent and understands what makes him special," I said.

She stared at me a long minute as if she couldn't comprehend the fact that I was complimenting her. When she

24

finally looked away, I saw her expression soften.

"We both took piano as kids, but Josh was way more into it than I was. I thought it was boring compared to skating." She toyed with the cuff of her blazer. "Josh used to learn every song I asked him to. He loved the challenge."

Now we're getting somewhere.

I pulled my knees up and rested my arms on them. "It never stops amazing me how he can listen to a song and learn it so quickly."

"Not only that, but he can remember it years later. He has a musical genius mind."

"He really does. I think the way he understands music so well is what's going to make him a top choreographer one day."

"I always knew he could be an amazing choreographer. Even when we were kids he would come up with ideas that were totally fresh and new."

I cocked my head to one side. "Well, how about that. We've talked for two minutes without any insults."

Her lips pressed into their familiar scowl. "Don't think that makes us BFFs now. I still think you and Josh skating together is a terrible idea."

She hadn't said Josh and I dating was a terrible idea. Was that a small improvement?

"I get you don't want him to skate with anyone else," I said. "You were the only partner he'd ever had. But no one can take away what you guys accomplished. No one can take away your Olympic experience."

"That's right. And I don't see you and Josh getting to the Olympics anyway."

I smiled a little and pressed my fingers to my forehead. "After tonight, I just want to get through an entire program."

Stephanie's phone vibrated, and her face lightened as she looked at the screen and answered the call.

"I have to tell you what happened." She scrambled to put

on her boots and then walked toward the hallway. "It's been the most awful night."

Stephanie's voice drifted farther away, and I slid down in my chair and used my jacket as a pillow against the wall. As I watched the *Friends* episode I'd seen a bazillion times, my eyelids grew droopier, and I gave in to the exhausting day. The next thing I felt was a hard poke on my arm.

"Wake up," I heard as I slowly opened my eyes.

Stephanie was standing beside my chair, and daylight filled the waiting room. I removed my smashed face from my makeshift pillow and rubbed my eyes. My hands came away with smudges of glittery eye shadow. I'd forgotten I was still wearing my stage makeup.

"The nurse said we can see Josh," Stephanie said and gave me a wrinkled-nose once-over. "You might want to look in the mirror first."

I lifted my eyebrows. I would've expected her to let me walk around looking like a hot mess. Perhaps we really were making headway.

After I did my best to freshen up in the restroom, Stephanie and I found Josh's room and tentatively pushed open the heavy door. Josh was in the bed closest to the door, poking at his breakfast, and an elderly man slept in the other bed.

"Hey," I whispered.

"Hey." Josh put down his fork. "You don't have to whisper. He can't hear even when he's awake."

"How are you feeling?" I rubbed his arm.

He pushed away his tray. "Better than last night."

He still sounded groggy, but he looked more alert. After seeing him unconscious on the ice, I didn't want to stop staring at his gorgeous eyes.

Stephanie peered at the watery scrambled eggs. "Those look gross."

"I can't handle food right now. The doctor said that's

common after a concussion." Josh looked from me to Stephanie and back again. "Did you come here together?"

"We stayed here all night," Stephanie said proudly.

"Just you two?"

"Yep, and look…" I twirled around. "No scars."

Stephanie rolled her eyes.

"Steph, can I talk to Court for a minute?" Josh asked.

She frowned, and he said, "Just for a minute."

She huffed and took her time leaving the room, and when the door shut Josh grasped my hand.

"I wanted to ask you… I don't remember what happened with the lift," he said.

I didn't want to remember either. If I could permanently erase that memory from my brain, I would be ecstatic.

"We just lost our balance. It all happened so quickly."

"Thank God you're okay." His voice became huskier.

"Only because of you. You held onto me and broke my fall."

"I couldn't let anything happen to you."

I sat on the bed and swallowed hard to stave off the tears. "When you blacked out… I've never been so scared in my life."

"I'm so sorry you had to go through that." Josh massaged my back.

I shook my head. "I don't want to think about it. I just want to help you heal and feel better."

"The doctor said I can't do any strenuous physical or mental activity until I'm symptom-free. So, basically I have to sit around and veg out."

"I can definitely help with that. We can watch lots of movies and listen to music, and I'll do whatever you need. I'll be a great nurse."

"Do you give sponge baths?" His smile was the biggest I'd seen since the accident.

I laughed. "I'd love to do that, but it would probably lead

to a certain strenuous physical activity."

He hummed softly in agreement. "That's very true."

"We should probably let Stephanie back in. I think we had a tiny breakthrough last night, so I don't want to ruin it."

"Okay... just one more thing." His face grew serious, and he locked our fingers together. "I love you... so much... and I promise I'll be back on the ice with you soon."

I caressed his cheek and ran my hand down to his chest, stopping on his heart. "I love you, too, and there's no rush."

He pulled me close, and I rested my head on his shoulder. My lips brushed his neck with a sweet kiss.

"I'll wait for you as long as you need."

Chapter Four

A few raindrops splattered on my nose as I walked through Mrs. Cassar's garden to the pool house. I knocked and opened the unlocked door, and I called Josh's name when I didn't see him.

There weren't many places he could go in the small space where I wouldn't spot him. French doors separated the bedroom from the tiny living room/kitchen combination. I went into the bedroom and saw the bathroom was dark, so I took off my jacket and went back to the kitchen. The door opened, and Josh came in carrying a brown paper bag.

"Hey, did you go out?" I asked.

He set the bag on the miniscule counter space. "No, Mrs. Cassar picked up some groceries for me."

"I could've done that for you."

"I didn't want to bother you."

"It's no bother. I know it sucks not being able to drive."

He didn't look up from where he was putting away the groceries, and I realized he hadn't kissed me hello. He *always* kissed me hello.

"Did you have any headaches today?" I lightly rubbed

his back.

"Not so far."

"I was thinking maybe you could have dinner with me at the restaurant before my shift. You can get a ride home with Mrs. Cassar later." She always ate there on Thursday nights, so I knew I could count on her.

Josh didn't say anything; he seemed more interested in the jar of peanut butter he was holding. He hadn't left his house in the four days we'd been back from Portland, and I thought a quiet Thursday night at the restaurant would be a good place to start. The doctor had prescribed plenty of rest, but he hadn't said Josh couldn't go out in public.

"I just thought you might be going stir crazy in here." I laughed a little to try to lighten what felt like an unsettling mood.

"Yeah... that sounds good," he said, though not very enthusiastically.

"Great!" I said with enough enthusiasm for both of us.

He looked down at his T-shirt and sweats. "Guess I should change."

As he walked past me into the bedroom, he stripped off his shirt, and I eyed him every step of the way. From his hard pecs to his rippled abs, there was good reason to swoon. I leaned against the fridge and continued to watch Josh as he stood in front of the closet. I missed the warmth of his body covering mine and the feel of his corded muscles under my palms. But his recovery was most important, and we'd have lots of time to make up for the lost nights. I shivered just thinking how good making up was going to be.

Josh chose a blue button-down shirt and jeans and went into the bathroom, so my show was over. I hoped getting him out of the house might make him feel more normal. Sitting around all day had to be depressing for someone who was used to a full schedule of activity. He obviously couldn't skate, and he'd also had to cancel his students' piano lessons. Per the doctor's orders, all he'd been able to do was watch TV, listen to music, and do light reading. Em and Sergei had handled most of the media requests, so Josh had only needed to do a few phone interviews about the accident.

He came out in his new set of clothes, and the sweet, sexy scent of his cologne teased my nose. I put my arms around his waist and tilted my head to look up at him.

"You're the hottest date a girl could ask for," I said.

His lips barely curled into a smile, and he gave my shoulders a gentle squeeze before scooting toward his jacket. "A truly hot date would be able to drive his own car."

Was that what was bothering him? Being dependent on me?

"You'll be back behind the wheel soon. The doctor will probably clear you when you see him next week."

"Hope so," he mumbled as he zipped up his jacket.

I slowly put on my own and searched my purse for my keys. On the ride to the restaurant, I got Josh talking more when I asked him which movie he'd watched that day. He described the plot of *The Blind Side*, and we were still discussing it when we entered the dining room. Opening wasn't for another hour, so only a few employees were there, my friend Meredith being one of them. She saw us and gave Josh a hug, which he stiffly returned.

"Welcome back," she said.

"I'm just here for dinner."

"You're lucky Ronnie's not here or he'd try to put you to work."

Josh shoved his hands in his pockets. "Soon."

The restaurant's chef cooked for the staff before the dinner shift, and that night he'd made shrimp pasta. Josh and I took our plates and sat at a table by the large windows. The view of Nantucket Sound was hidden by streaks of rain on the glass.

I twirled the vermicelli around my fork and tried to think

of something to break the silence that had set in. "I'm guessing your family isn't flying out for Thanksgiving?"

"I doubt it."

"Well, my mom will love having you over for dinner. She makes enough food to feed an army even though we're a family of three."

Josh stabbed a shrimp with his fork. "The most I've ever seen my mom do in the kitchen is open a take-out container."

"So she never helped Stephanie make her vegan meals?"

He shook his head as he chewed. "When Steph became a vegan a few years ago, my mom wasn't exactly supportive. She told her if she wanted to be skinnier, she should go on a diet."

"Sadly, that doesn't surprise me at all," I said as I lifted my glass of water to my lips.

I noticed Josh had been glancing behind me while we talked, so I turned and found the likely center of his attention — the piano.

"It would probably be okay for you to play a little." I pointed my thumb at the baby grand. "You've been getting a lot of rest. You could play something easy like... I don't know... 'Over the Rainbow?'"

I gave him a coy smile. It was tradition that Josh played the song, one of my favorites, every Thursday night.

"Why would I play that?" His brow furrowed.

A cold chill raced down my spine. *Oh my God. He doesn't remember.*

"You... you don't..." I sputtered quietly.

His face cracked into a sly grin. "You thought I had amnesia."

I gaped at him and shoved his leg with my foot under the table. "Don't joke about stuff like that!"

"Sorry, sorry." He held up his hands.

I supposed I should be thankful he was joking around. Maybe that meant he was feeling more like himself. Playing the piano would only help that even more.

"Now that you're done scaring the crap out of me, are you gonna play my song or what?" I said.

He wiped his mouth on his napkin and pushed back his chair. I followed him over to the piano and stood beside it as he sat on the bench. He cracked his knuckles and gazed at the keys for a minute before setting his fingers on them. But he still didn't play. He picked up his hands and shifted them, continuing to stare at the keys. A tiny vee had formed above his nose.

Is he messing with me again?

He pulled his hands back but kept his eyes on the piano. "I can't... I can't remember it."

The dazed look on his face told me he wasn't kidding. Was this normal after a concussion? I'd read about short-term memory issues, but Josh hadn't shown signs of any type of memory loss so far.

"Maybe you just need help getting started. The sheet music is in the bench—"

"I don't need the sheet music," he barked. "I've played this song fifty thousand times."

I took a step back from the piano. Josh never raised his voice to me. He never raised his voice to anyone except his mom and sister when they were being ugly to me. I didn't know how to respond, so I went with a calm approach, which I thought might help.

"Do you want to try another song?" I asked.

He raked his fingers roughly through his hair. "I'm looking at the keys, and I don't even know where to start."

My heart rate had become elevated with worry, but I didn't want Josh to know this was freaking me out, too. I had to be the voice of reason because he was in full-blown panic mode.

"You probably just need a little more time. You're still recovering." I tentatively approached him and put my hand on his arm. "Let's go finish our dinner."

"I've lost my appetite," he said.

If I'd thought he looked down before, it was nothing compared to how glum he looked now. I moved behind him and circled my arms around his shoulders, giving him a warm hug, and I leaned over so we were cheek to cheek.

"This is just temporary," I said softly.

It has to be, right?

He didn't appear to be getting up from his spot, so I slowly pulled away and went back to the table to clear our dishes. I'd lost my appetite, too.

When I returned from the kitchen, Josh had taken his usual seat at the long bar. At least one thing had gone back to normal. I tied a black apron over my black pants and got to work behind the bar, preparing it for the dinner crowd.

I kept a close eye on Josh as I worked. He still looked pretty dazed as he sipped his water. I was glad when the doors opened for business and Mrs. Cassar arrived shortly after. Her sense of humor could bring anyone out of a funk.

She left her umbrella by the door and perched on the stool next to Josh's. I snatched the bottle of merlot and had Mrs. Cassar's glass filled before she got settled.

"Thank you, Dear," she said and gave Josh a long look. "Are you feeling okay? You look pale."

He rested his arms on the bar and pinched the bridge of his nose. "My brain's not feeling so hot."

Mrs. Cassar's gray eyes swung to me with alarm, and I said, "He tried to play the piano and had some trouble remembering."

"I couldn't remember *anything*," he corrected.

"Well, Joshua, you bashed your head on a block of ice. Of course things will be muddled up there." She patted his back. "Give it time. You're going to be just fine."

Meredith placed her small tray on the bar. "Court, can I get a vodka tonic?"

I lingered a moment before gathering the bottles I needed for the drink. I stayed busy the next hour, so I only caught bits of Josh and Mrs. Cassar's conversation. I didn't hear much of the standard laughter. When Mrs. Cassar went to the ladies' room, I refilled Josh's water and included a smile. He looked up at me, his eyes filled with uneasiness.

"What if I forgot how to skate?" he asked.

"You haven't. You've been doing it for too many years—"

I stopped when I realized he'd been playing the piano just as long. But skating was more physical. His muscle memory would trump his mental memory, wouldn't it?

"I don't think you should worry about that," I said quickly.

"Josh!" our boss Ronnie bellowed as he came out of the kitchen. "You said you wouldn't be here."

"I just came for dinner. I'm about to head out."

"Stay and play a few songs. We need some life in here tonight."

I cringed on the inside as I waited for Josh's response. He gripped his glass tighter and kept his head down.

"I... I can't," he said.

"Come on, just thirty minutes. I know you—"

"I said I can't!" Josh jumped up from his stool and stormed out the door.

I stood motionless with the water pitcher frozen in my hand, while Ronnie's eyes doubled in size. "What was that?" he asked.

"He's just... he's upset because he doesn't remember how to play right now. It must be an aftereffect of the concussion."

"Damn, I wouldn't have bugged the kid if I'd known."

"I'm sorry, I didn't know you were here or I would've given you a heads-up."

He drummed his fingers on the bar. "It's just temporary, right?"

"I'm sure it is." I tried to make myself sound more confident than I felt.

Ronnie left to circle the room and greet the customers, and Mrs. Cassar soon joined me and asked, "Where's Joshua?"

"Ronnie asked him to play a few songs, obviously not knowing his... condition, and he blew up and walked out."

"Blew up? Joshua?" Her eyes grew as big as Ronnie's had.

"It surprised me, too."

She glanced at the door. "What's he doing — standing in the rain?"

"I don't know. Can you go check on him?"

She slipped on her coat and picked up her umbrella at the door. When neither she nor Josh returned after ten minutes, I assumed they'd gone home. Which meant Josh had left without saying goodbye.

Near the end of my shift I checked my phone and had no messages. I pulled up Josh's number and typed a text.

Me: *Are you still up?*

I stared at the screen until it went black, and I dropped it into my apron pocket. By the time I closed down the bar, I had a reply waiting.

Josh: *Yeah*

Me: *Do you want some company?*

I didn't receive an answer until I was inside my car, buckling my seat belt.

Josh: *I wouldn't be great company.*

My heart pinched. I hated the idea of him being alone with nothing but worrisome thoughts filling his head.

Me: *We don't have to talk. We can just watch a movie. I'm skating the late session tomorrow, so I can stay over.*

Josh: *I haven't been sleeping well, so you wouldn't get much rest.*

I put my head back against the seat. *Take a hint, Court. He doesn't want you there. No matter how much you want to be there for him.*

Me: *Okay. I'll stop by after I leave the rink tomorrow.*

I waited for a response but got none. At least he hadn't told me not to come.

When I reached Em and Sergei's house, I quietly let myself in and turned off the kitchen light they'd left on for me. I took off my shoes and padded up the stairs to my room, where I grabbed my pajamas and headed straight for the shower. With the smell of food washed from my hair and skin, I snuggled under the thick comforter with my laptop and typed what I'd been worried about all night.

Effects of a concussion

The search engine spit out thousands of hits with something called Post-Concussion Syndrome or PCS for short. I clicked on one of the reputable medical sites and began to read.

Symptoms include headaches, anxiety, mood swings, irritability, loss of concentration and memory, insomnia... usually occur within first seven to ten days and can last weeks... may sometimes persist for months or even years.

Years??

I chewed on my thumbnail as I clicked on another site. *That's worst-case scenario. Don't go there.*

I found more of the same information on other sites, so I tried searching for instances of people who had suffered a concussion and had forgotten how to play a musical instrument. I couldn't find anything, but there were many examples of patients who had problems with cognitive skills. Some indeed lasting years.

I shut the laptop and shoved it to the empty side of the bed. *Don't get yourself worked up. Every case is different. Josh could start to feel better in a few days.*

But I was officially concerned.

Chapter Five

"Your turn, Coco." Quinn shook my knee.

I looked up from the Candy Land game board at four-year-old Quinn and her twin brother Alex. I'd spaced out somewhere between Peppermint Forest and Gumdrop Pass. My mind was on Josh and his doctor appointment. Em and Sergei had gone with him, so I was babysitting the twins. The house smelled like the pumpkin pie Em had baked for her family's Thanksgiving feast the next day.

"Let's see if I can get lucky," I said as I picked a card from the pile.

Alex leaned into me to see my card. "You go two blue squares."

"That's right." I moved my gingerbread man marker across the board and cuddled Alex to my side. "Better watch out. I'm catching up to you."

He shook his little blond head. "You not gonna catch me."

"I gonna beat you *and* Coco," Quinn announced.

The side door from the garage opened, and Josh, Em, and Sergei entered the kitchen, none of them wearing the smiles I'd hoped to see.

"Josh!" Quinn scrambled up from the living room carpet and ran toward him.

He crouched to hug her, and Quinn threw herself around him, almost tipping him backward.

"Be careful, Sweetie," Em said.

Quinn looked at Josh and petted his hair. "Your head hurt?"

He smiled a little. "It's getting better."

Alex raced over and latched onto Josh's arm. "Come see my new truck, Josh."

"Let's give him some space to breathe, okay?" Em said.

"It's fine," Josh said.

He let Alex lead him to the stairs, and Quinn followed right on their heels. Meanwhile, I joined Em and Sergei in the kitchen.

"What did the doctor say?" I asked.

"He did some testing, and he wants Josh to take it easy a while longer," Sergei said. "He's encouraged the headaches are fewer and farther between. Next Friday he'll evaluate him again to see if he can start driving and doing light workouts."

Em opened one of the cabinets and pulled out a large skillet. "I told Josh even if he gets cleared to skate, I don't want him on the ice without Sergei and me there. He can start on the bike in the gym."

"Why won't you be there?"

"We're going to China right after the Christmas show, remember?"

"Oh, yeah." I'd forgotten they had a junior team competing in the Grand Prix Final, plus Sergei's sixteen-year-old daughter Liza had qualified at the senior level.

"Did the doctor say anything about Josh's memory and not being able to play the piano?" I asked.

"He suggested Josh should start slowly and do simple lessons like he gives his students. He thinks it could help him remember and recover the skill he already has."

"Does he think there's any chance he won't recover it?" I gripped the edge of the granite island.

Em stopped in the middle of gathering ingredients from the fridge and came over to touch my arm. "He's been playing for so long. I know it's going to come back to him."

"I think it's really stressing him out, and that's just making things worse," I said.

"The doctor did say stress can lengthen the recovery, so anything you can do to get Josh to relax would be a huge help," Em said.

"We tried to focus on all the positives with him, but he was pretty wound up at the doctor," Sergei said.

Josh had been so moody the past week that I didn't know if anything could relax him. And from the tense look on his face as he descended the stairs, spending time with the jabbering twins wasn't the answer.

"Coco, come finish the game," Quinn said.

"You play too, Josh." Alex tugged on his hand.

Josh loved playing with Quinn and Alex, but probably not so much right now. They weren't exactly the best medicine for a headache.

"Josh needs to rest, so I'm gonna bring him home," I said.

"You're sure you don't want to stay for dinner?" Em held up a package of tortillas. "It's taco night."

"Thanks, but I am kinda tired," Josh said.

"But we have to finish the game," Quinn whined.

"I'll take Court's place." Sergei stretched his long legs over the carpet. "Which marker is hers?"

"She green," Alex said.

I turned to Josh. "I just need to get my bag upstairs."

"Your bag?"

"I figured I'd stay over since we're driving to my parents' tomorrow morning."

He ushered me away from Sergei and the twins. "I've

told you I don't sleep well. I'm up and down all night."

"I don't mind. I'll take a restless night of sleep if it means being next to you." I fiddled with the zipper on his jacket. "I miss you."

He avoided my gaze and hesitated a few moments. "Okay."

A little jab nicked my heart. I'd never thought I would have to talk Josh into letting me spend the night with him. I knew he wasn't himself, but it was still hard to feel him being so distant.

I hurried to my room and back before Josh could change his mind. He was silent all the way down Route Twenty-Eight, his head back and his eyes closed. When we reached Hyannis Port and I drove onto Mrs. Cassar's quiet street, he finally came alive.

"I have to get back on the ice soon if we're going to make it to nationals," he said.

"We have two months. That's definitely doable."

"But we don't have two months. Even if I'm cleared to skate next Friday, Em and Sergei said I can't until they get back. That means the earliest I could start is almost three weeks from now."

I pulled into Mrs. Cassar's double driveway and shut off the engine. "We'd still have enough time to get ready. Don't start stressing yet."

His anxiety-filled silence showed he was continuing to worry, though. We walked around the main house to the backyard, and once we were inside he said, "You know Em and Sergei aren't going to let me do any of the hard stuff right away, so we'll really have a month at best to fully train our programs."

"We'll take it one day at a time." I set my bag beside Josh's big keyboard in the living room. "Making sure you're healthy is the most important thing."

He tossed his jacket over the couch. "We can't miss

nationals. Not after all the work we've put in."

"Stressing yourself out isn't going to help you get better." I put my hands on his shoulders and felt just how tense he was. "You're all knotted up."

He let out a long, slow breath. "Playing the piano always helped." His eyes flashed sadly at the keyboard. "Can't do that anymore."

I took both his hands in mine. "Come sit."

I brought him to the sofa and turned him so I could sit behind him. Returning my hands to his shoulders, I massaged them with just the right amount of pressure. At first Josh remained rigid, but slowly his tight muscles began to loosen. He bent his head forward and groaned softly, and I scooted nearer to him. It felt so good to be so close to him and touching him. My lips stamped a tiny kiss on the nape of his neck, and my fingers kneaded their way down his back. I slipped one hand under his shirt, meeting his smooth skin, and he quickly jumped up from the couch.

"Court, don't."

"I was just trying to relax you."

He backed farther away. "That's not going to help me relax."

"I'm sorry. I wanted to get your mind off everything—"

"When you touch me like that, there's only one thing on my mind, and it's yet another thing I can't do right now."

My eyes dropped to the sofa. "I didn't mean to…"

"I know. I'm not mad at you. I'm just…" He rubbed his forehead. "Frustrated."

The silence that followed couldn't be more awkward, and it seemed to stretch on for days. When I couldn't take it anymore, I went to the refrigerator.

"Do you want the leftover chicken?" I asked.

The tension hovered around us as we ate and continued afterward as we watched TV. We sat side by side, but there may as well have been a moat between us. There was none of the cuddling we usually did. I longed to get cozy against him but didn't want him to yell at me again.

Josh let me take a shower first, and when I came out of the bathroom I saw he'd moved his pillow to the sofa.

"You don't have to sleep out here," I said. "I'm not going to touch you if that's what you're worried about."

"No, I just don't want to keep you up with all my tossing and turning."

"You shouldn't be all cramped on this small sofa. It's not good for your head and neck."

He turned down the TV volume with the remote. "I'm up most of the night, so it's not like I'm sleeping in one spot."

I leaned against the bedroom door frame. "Did you tell the doctor about your insomnia?"

"He said to let him know next week if it's still bad."

I frowned. It had already been bad for two weeks. Wasn't that long enough to warrant a solution of some kind?

"I told you I don't mind you tossing and turning next to me," I said. "Just come lay down. You never know — tonight might be different."

"I doubt it." He went to the sink and poured a glass of water. "I'm going to end up out here watching TV anyway, so it's better if I just camp here now."

I was obviously not going to convince him otherwise. I pushed off from the door frame and shuffled over to Josh in my big fuzzy slippers.

"Guess this is goodnight, then," I said.

He set down his glass and inched closer to me, and I buzzed with anticipation. His lips parted, his eyes on mine, and then... his kiss landed on my forehead. I sighed with resignation and retreated to the bedroom, where I curled up under the blanket and settled for only Josh's scent surrounding me.

****

43

Even though I had the entire bed to myself, I didn't sleep soundly. I kept dreaming about skating, but I couldn't remember seeing Josh in any of my fitful dreams. Josh was dragging, too, as we got ready in the morning, and we were both bleary-eyed as we traveled to Boston.

Mom welcomed us to the apartment with long hugs, and my mouth watered from the smell of the roasting turkey. I gave Dad a kiss and checked out the festive autumn tablescape Mom had created on the small dining table. My parents had been forced to sell my childhood home on the Cape after Dad had lost his job, and holidays in the apartment just hadn't felt the same. But Mom always did the best she could with her crafting skills in the limited space.

"How was your doctor's appointment, Josh?" Mom asked.

"I'm still not allowed to do anything of substance, so it wasn't the outcome I was hoping for."

"Well, you don't want to rush it," Mom said as she placed the silverware on the table. "Time is your friend."

"Not if we want to compete at nationals," Josh said.

"I thought we weren't going to worry about that," I said, failing to hide my exasperation.

"It's hard not to worry with the clock ticking down." Josh sounded just as annoyed.

Mom and Dad were staring at us, and there weren't many options for privacy in the place.

"Can we talk in my room for a minute?" I said to Josh.

He silently agreed, and I shut the bedroom door behind us. I didn't stay there often, so Mom had stored most of her craft supplies there. Josh and I stepped around boxes to stand in front of the bed.

"If we can't get ready in time for nationals, it won't be the end of the world," I said.

"I thought competing there was just as important to you as it is to me."

"It is but not at the expense of your health. I don't understand why you're so worked up over this. Is it because of your family? Do you feel like we have to be at nationals to prove to them you made the right decision? About skating with me?"

"No, it's about proving to you that *you* made the right decision." Josh lowered his gaze to the carpet. "I haven't exactly been the best partner so far."

"Because we've had some bad luck with injuries?"

"It just hasn't been what I wanted for us... what I promised you." He looked up at me, his tired eyes so troubled.

I placed my hands on both sides of his face. "I love being your partner, and I meant what I said at the hospital. I will happily wait for you to get better. As long as it takes."

I hugged him and felt how knotted his body was again. Massages were apparently out of the question, so I would have to find another way to help relieve his tension.

We returned to the living room and watched the Macy's parade while Mom put the finishing touches on dinner. Josh excused himself to call his family, and when I went to wash my hands I could hear his conversation in my room.

"Steph? Hey." After a short pause he said, "I'm feeling great. I should be back on the ice next week."

Feeling great? Since when? And what was that chipper tone in his voice? I hadn't heard that in forever. I also hadn't heard the news that he would be skating the next week.

I waited for him at the end of the hallway and questioned him as soon as he came out of my room. "Why did you lie to your sister?"

He shoved his phone hard into his pocket. "Were you eavesdropping?"

"I happened to hear you when I went to the bathroom. Why didn't you tell her the truth?"

"If she knew the truth, all I'd get is more flack about skating with you and how I've totally screwed up my life."

"Maybe so, but it's better to be honest with them in case—"

"In case what? I don't get better?"

Anxious pressure rose in my chest. Even after a week of dealing with snippy Josh, I still wasn't used to it. Every time he snapped at me I felt myself on the verge of either tears or losing my cool. I took a deep breath and reminded myself to be patient. It wasn't Josh's fault his moods were all out of whack.

"You're going to get better," I said. "I was just going to say we don't know how long it will take, and you can't keep lying to your family."

"They won't know the difference. Steph's the only one who's been checking up on me. My dad's called once since the accident. I could be dead over here for all he cares."

I winced at the harshness of his statement. "Josh, don't say that."

"It's true."

Mom peeked into the hallway. "Dinner's ready."

"We'll be there in a sec," I said.

"We shouldn't let the turkey get cold." Josh walked around me.

"Wait," I said, but he kept going.

Mom looked at me with concern. "Everything okay?"

I thought about what we were celebrating that day and how I should be thankful Josh was there with me, walking and talking... even if it was grumpy talking. His condition could have been so much worse with the fall he'd taken. *Patience*, I repeated to myself.

I nodded and forced a tiny smile. "It will be."

Chapter Six

If I never had to hear "Rockin' Around the Christmas Tree" again it would be too soon. Em was making us rehearse the Christmas show opening number for the five hundredth time. She and Josh had choreographed all the show numbers, and with him being out of commission, she'd been stressing more than usual. The event was only one day away, so this was our final rehearsal and Em's final chance to direct the controlled chaos. Josh and I obviously wouldn't be able to skate our planned program in the show, but I was still in the opening and also had a duet with Liza.

Em finally dismissed us, and Liza skated over to me while braiding her long, raven ponytail.

"Did you see Josh come in?" she asked.

I looked back at the double doors to the lobby. "No. When?"

"It was during the last run-through. He went up to the lounge." She tied a rubber band around the end of her braid. "He must be stoked he can drive again."

I had thought he would be, but when I'd talked to him on the phone after his appointment that morning, he had still sounded down. He'd said he might stop by the rink, but I hadn't counted on it.

"I'm gonna go find him," I said before gliding to the ice door.

After I changed out of my skates, I climbed the narrow staircase to the lounge and found Josh surrounded by skaters and moms. He hadn't been at the rink since the accident, so questions were flying at him. I could hear lots of comments of "It was so terrible!" and "Do you remember falling?" With his hands stuffed in his pockets and his eyes darting around the room, Josh looked like he was undergoing a painful interrogation rather than a friendly conversation.

"Hey, I need to steal this guy." I put my arm around Josh, steering him away from the mob.

As we walked downstairs he let out a breath, and I asked, "You okay?"

He rubbed the back of his neck. "They all bombarded me at once."

"Everyone is just happy to see you."

We went out to the rink, and Josh stopped a few feet short of the boards. He stared at the ice, looking even more uneasy than he had in the lounge. He'd been so gung-ho about training again that I hadn't even thought about him having any reservations.

"Are you thinking about the accident?" I asked.

He took a hard swallow. "Just umm... just ready to get back."

He didn't look like someone raring to go, but I didn't want to question him and make him irritated with me, which was happening too often lately.

"Only ten more days," I said. "Em said as soon as they're back from China."

With a stiff nod he turned away from the ice, and he dropped onto a chair by the lobby doors, his knees bouncing nervously. *Okay, I have to say something.*

"Did you talk to the doctor about your insomnia, your anxiousness..." I asked.

"He made an appointment for me to see a neuropsychologist, but I don't need another doctor. I need to be able to skate and to work."

"I think you should go. The pyschologist might be able to help you deal with all the issues you're having."

"She can't help me with my biggest issue, which is how I'm not going to have any money if I can't remember how to play the piano soon. I really don't want to dip into my trust fund and have my parents say 'I told you so.'"

"You might remember how to play sooner if you let the doctor treat you."

"Hi, Josh!" One of the skater moms interrupted us. "It's so good to have you back. You gave us all such a scare. I've seen some bad falls but never anything like that. I don't know how you—"

"I have to get going." Josh shot to his feet. "Sorry, it's good to see you."

He bolted for the door, and I left the befuddled woman behind to chase after him. I called his name, and he turned with one foot out the door.

"I can't listen to any more talk about how horrific our fall was," he said.

"You know how people are. It'll stop once you've been back a few days."

He stepped farther outside. "I need to get out of here before anyone else catches me."

Frosty air blew into the lobby, and I hugged my arms to my chest. "Are you coming to the restaurant tonight?"

"I'm not sure. I'll text you."

He rushed out, and I waved feebly at the closed door. My throat ached from the swell of tears that needed to be released. One of the things I loved about Josh was the way he looked at me — how he made me feel so wanted and adored without speaking a word. But I saw none of that when he looked at me now. There was a dark cloud covering his eyes.

Blinking back the tears, I spun toward the locker room and smacked into Em. We both yelped and spit out apologies, and then she took a closer look at me.

"What's wrong?" she asked.

I dabbed the corners of my eyes and shook my head. "I don't know how to help Josh."

She linked her arm through mine. "I think we should get some chocolate and talk."

She bought us each a cup of Dippin' Dots from the machine in the lobby, and we sat at a table in the empty snack bar. I spooned a big helping of the frozen treat into my mouth, and it numbed my tongue.

"Sergei said the doctor wants Josh to see a neuropsychologist," Em said.

"He doesn't want to go. You'd think he'd want answers and some help getting better. I thought getting the news that he can skate and drive again would cheer him up, but he's still not happy."

"Being back at the rink didn't help?"

"I think it made it worse. He was so jumpy when people tried to talk to him about the accident."

Em's eyebrows bent with worry. "He might be nervous about getting back on the ice."

"He hasn't said he is, but he's not saying much to me these days." I swirled my spoon around my cup. "He barely looks at me."

"You know he loves you more than anything."

"I know. It's just hard being around him and not feeling that from him at all. I'm trying not to let it hurt, but..." My voice caught as tears snuck up on me again.

Em leaned toward me. "I'll get Sergei to talk to him about seeing the new doctor. We'll all do whatever we can to get him through this."

There had to be something the doctor could do to help Josh — some medicine, some therapy, something. He couldn't go on like this. The longer he was stuck in this dark place, the more I feared he wouldn't be able to get out.

****

I coughed and waved my hand in front of my face. The hair spray fumes in the locker room were at their pre-show high. There wasn't an inch of free space in the room with all of us jammed inside, doing our last-minute primping. I squeezed between bodies for a peek at the mirror, and I pulled a loose stone from the side of my sparkly silver dress.

"Court!" Em pushed through the crowd to get to me. "Where's Josh?"

"He's not here?"

"I don't see him out there. I was going to ask him to take a bow at the end of the show for all the work he did."

I hesitated a moment as a remote possibility crossed my mind, but I shook it off. "Maybe he's just running late."

Even with all Josh's moodiness, he wouldn't bail on the show. Besides being there to support me, he knew Em and all the kids he'd worked with wanted him there.

"Em, my dad needs you," Liza called from the door.

I followed Em out to the rink so I could look for Josh. Clomping in my skate guards, I walked the length of the packed bleachers and stopped when I saw Mrs. Cassar.

"Was Josh still home when you left?" I asked.

"His car was there. I assumed he was leaving soon."

I sent a worried glance at the rink entrance. What if something bad had happened? Josh had only been back behind the wheel for one day, and a light snow had been falling when I'd arrived at the rink.

"I'm gonna call him," I said and hurried to the locker room.

I took my phone into the lobby to get away from the din of the crowd, and my pulse sped up as Josh's phone rang and rang. When he finally answered I exhaled.

"Hey, are you on your way?" I asked.

Silence met my question, and I said louder, "Josh?"

"I'm not coming."

I stood speechless a few seconds. "Are you not feeling well?"

"I can't handle all those people. I'm sorry."

"There you are." Liza rushed into the lobby. "It's show time."

I was still gaping at the phone, and I felt an explosion building within me. Liza was frantically motioning for me to go with her, so I pressed the phone screen hard to end the call, not bothering to say goodbye.

The lights had dimmed, and Em was standing on the ice under the spotlight, welcoming everyone. I asked Sergei to hold my phone, and I gathered with the other skaters in the opening number. My heart was still pounding from my conversation with Josh. I shook out my arms and took deep breaths to calm myself, but I couldn't shake the irritation. *How could he not show up?*

Sergei directed us to take the ice, and I plastered a smile on my face. We'd practiced the number so many times that I skated mechanically through it, my mind still on Josh's absence. I needed to get my head in the game for my duet with Liza, though. The choreography for that program was more complex, and we had to do two jumps. Liza, a jumping machine, was going to nail them for sure, so I didn't want to flub them and mar our performance.

I stretched and paced beside the boards to stay warm while the younger skaters performed, and Em slipped over to me between her emcee duties.

"Did you find Josh?" she asked.

"He didn't come," I said.

She must have heard the iciness in my tone because she didn't ask any questions. She just rubbed my shoulder and went back to her spot at the microphone.

I met Liza at the ice door, and she put her hand up for a high five. "Ready to be awesome?"

I slapped her hand and shut my mental door on everything except the ice in front of us. "Totally."

Em introduced us, and we skated to the center of the rink, where we stood back to back. When "O Holy Night" by John Legend began to play, we pushed off in opposite directions, me shimmering in silver and Liza in gold. Being in the spotlight with the music playing, my adrenaline kicked into high gear, and I sped around the corner of the rink. I stretched into a spiral, and Liza flew past me in matching position.

As the cool breeze fanned across my face, I wished Josh was there to lift me high into the air so I could truly feel like I was flying. I missed the rush of excitement that I felt every time we did a lift. He wasn't there, though. Not on the ice and not even in the audience. My annoyance with him bubbled up again, and I quickly refocused on the double Axel ahead. I jumped up and spun two-and-a-half times, and Liza did the same beside me. We landed in sync on the high piano note just as Josh had choreographed it.

I lost myself in the soulful rendition of the song and was sad when we struck our ending poses. I'd had so few chances to perform lately that I didn't want to leave the ice. Knowing Josh and I might miss nationals, our last chance to compete that season, made me even more reluctant to take my bows.

After Liza and I exited to a rousing ovation, I changed out of my costume and watched the rest of the show from the edge of the bleachers. Once the lights came up, everyone flocked to the tables filled with punch and Christmas cookies. I tried to disappear before I would get inundated with questions about Josh, but I didn't succeed. I got trapped next to the locker room, forced to make excuses for Josh being a no-show.

When I managed to escape, I grabbed my things, put my head down, and snuck out the side door. With my car pointed toward Hyannis Port, I started the conversation I needed to have with Josh in my head, and it only got me more riled up.

Tiny snowflakes stuck to my hair as I rapped my knuckles on Josh's door. He opened it and looked surprised to see me. Had he really thought we weren't going to talk about this?

I barged into the kitchen and pulled off my gloves. "I can't believe you bailed."

"You saw how everyone was all over me yesterday. It would've been ten times worse tonight with so many people there."

"You couldn't just suck it up and talk to them? To be there for me? For all the kids who wanted to show you the hard work they put into your programs?"

He marched past me and sat on the couch, holding his head in his hands. "I couldn't breathe yesterday when they were all surrounding me."

I took a few steps toward him and softened my voice. "Josh, that's not normal."

"Don't you think I know that?" He snapped. "Why can't everyone just leave me alone?"

"Because we care about you! You haven't been yourself since the accident, and we're worried—"

"Well, stop. Stop worrying, stop trying to help. You can't."

Every harsh word he spoke made my stomach knot tighter. I'd never thought Josh could make me feel that way.

"Is that really what you want? To push away the people who love you?" I asked.

He pinched the bridge of his nose. "I just can't deal with this."

This meaning *me?* I didn't want to ask that question because it would hurt too much to hear the certain answer.

I gritted my teeth to settle my trembling chin. "Fine. If that's what you want, I'll leave you alone to figure it all out on your own. You let me know when you've done that."

I went out into the frigid night, and it didn't feel any colder than the air in Josh's house had been. I hurried down the stone path but stopped as my emotions battled inside me. I thought about going back, but what would that accomplish? Josh clearly didn't want me around, and I didn't think I could take any more of his frustration aimed at me. As much as I hated walking out on him, things were only going to get uglier between us if I stayed. I swiped my eyes and kept going, ignoring the pull on my heart that urged me to turn around.

Chapter Seven

With my phone cradled between my ear and my shoulder, I stirred the noodles boiling on Em's stove and waited for Mrs. Cassar to answer my call. Five days had passed since I'd seen Josh, so I had been checking in with Mrs. Cassar to make sure he was okay.

"Hello, Dear," she answered above the sound of people talking in the background.

"Are you at the restaurant?"

"It's Thursday night, isn't it?"

I smiled. "Yes, it is. I don't suppose Josh is with you?"

"No, I haven't been able to talk him into going out. He's been staying to himself."

My smile turned into a frown. The fact that he was still locked up in his house both worried and angered me. He couldn't hide there forever, hoping to get better.

I set down the wooden spoon and tore open the packet of powdered cheese. "Has he still been out of sorts?"

"When I talked to him this morning, he seemed more at ease… not about to jump out of his skin like he's been."

Not at ease enough to call me, though.

"He'll come to you soon, I'm sure." Mrs. Cassar appeared to read my mind. "He just needs to get himself together first."

I stirred the pasta again and blinked quickly as tears pricked my eyes. "I just miss him. This is the longest we've been apart in almost a year."

"I guarantee he misses you, too. If there's one thing I know about Joshua, there's nothing he wants more in this world than to be with you."

"I'd feel a lot more confident about that if I heard it from him. Things have been so off between us the past few weeks."

"Coco, we hungry," Alex said behind me.

I turned to see Quinn and him climbing onto chairs at the kitchen table.

"Dinner will be ready in a minute," I said loudly to clear the shakiness in my voice.

"You go feed the little ones," Mrs. Cassar said. "And keep your chin up. You'll hear from Joshua soon."

"Thanks for keeping an eye on him."

"Of course. I'd do anything for you two."

I thanked her again and put the phone on the granite island. After straining the noodles, I mixed the cheese powder with butter and milk and tossed everything together. Em had left meals in the freezer for me to heat up while she and Sergei were in China, but I had run out, so I'd made one of the few dishes my limited cooking skills could handle.

Alex dove into his bowl, but Quinn just stared at hers.

"This don't look like Mommy's mac and cheese," she said.

That's because Mommy is a gourmet cook who makes the pasta from scratch and grates the cheese herself.

"It's different, but it's still yummy," I said.

She wrinkled her nose and peered closer at the bowl. "Why it orange?"

"Just try it. I'm sure you'll like it."

"It's good," Alex said with a mouthful of noodles.

"See? Trust your brother," I said.

Quinn shook her head, bouncing her blond curls. "I don't like it."

"You haven't even tasted it."

"I don't wanna taste it." She folded her arms. "It's yucky."

I dropped my fork into my bowl with a loud clatter. I had enough problems in my life without dealing with a four-year-old's stubbornness.

"Quinn, you're not getting anything else to eat unless you try it, so either taste it or go hungry."

She continued to pout, not moving an inch. Meanwhile, Alex couldn't get the food into his mouth fast enough.

"If you don't eat, you're not watching the movie later," I said. "Alex and I will watch it together, and you'll be up in your room all by yourself."

Her bottom lip began to quiver.

"Uh-uh," I said. "The waterworks aren't going to get you anywhere, Missy. You know your mommy and daddy wouldn't fall for it."

The doorbell rang, and I kept an eye on the table as I went to answer the door. I didn't trust Quinn not to shovel some of her dinner into Alex's bowl to make it look like she had eaten it. I'd caught her doing that once. I looked through the front window, and my heart leapt at the sight of Josh on the front porch.

I opened the door, and he greeted me with a quiet, "Hey."

"Josh!" Quinn cried before I could get a word out.

Her chair scraped the tile floor, and I whipped around. "Do not move from that table until you start eating."

"Bad time?" Josh asked.

I looked back at him and motioned for him to come inside. "Quinn's insisting her dinner is yucky without even trying it."

He walked into the kitchen and leaned over Quinn's shoulder. "You don't want mac and cheese? That's the best."

I observed him closely. He looked *and* sounded more relaxed. More like himself.

"You want some?" I asked. "I have extra."

"Sure."

He sat beside me with his bowl, and Quinn watched as he chewed and hummed with satisfaction.

"You don't know what you're missing, Quinn," he said.

I smiled at hearing him tease her. Whatever he'd been up to the past week, it had definitely helped.

Quinn picked up her fork and poked at the noodles, and I reminded her, "You just have to try it, and you'll be able to watch the movie with us."

"You stay for the movie, Josh?" she asked.

He turned to me with expectant eyes, and I took that as another good sign. A week ago he would have avoided hanging out with the twins.

"You're welcome to stay if you feel up to it. We're watching *WALL-E*," I said.

"I'd love to," he said.

"Yay!" Quinn scooped up a few noodles and put them in her mouth. "Now can I watch the movie?"

"Chew and swallow, please," I said.

She did as I asked and went back for more.

"Not so yucky, is it?" I said and looked at Josh. "I plead with her to no avail, and you show up and she's chowing down."

"Must be my irresistible charm," he said with a tiny smile.

My heart soared again as I got another glimpse of my sweet Josh. The one I'd been missing so much.

We ate a few minutes in silence, but I couldn't hold back the questions any longer. I had to know what Josh had done to pull himself out of his funk.

"You seem to be feeling better," I said.

He took a sip of water. "I'm working on it. I saw the neuropsychologist."

"Oh, good."

"She gave me medication to help me sleep, and she suggested I meditate and do yoga to clear my head since I used to do hot yoga all the time."

"Mommy do yogi," Quinn said.

"Yes, she does," I said.

"I found some videos online so I can work out at home and save money," Josh said.

"It looks like it's really helping."

"It is." He toyed with his pasta and took a small bite. "Are you watching the twins until Em and Sergei get home?"

"No, Em's parents are coming to get them tomorrow."

"Then you should come over this weekend and do it with me."

My gulp of water went partially down my windpipe, and I coughed into my napkin.

"Yoga," Josh said with a knowing smile.

My stomach turned all fluttery. Oh, how I'd missed that feeling he gave me.

"Right." I cleared my throat.

"Grandma and Grandpa gonna take us to the froggie pond," Quinn said.

I laughed and corrected her, "Frog Pond."

She went on to ramble about the other things they were going to do in Boston, but I only caught bits and pieces. I was too busy still reveling in Josh's smile.

We all moved into the living room after dinner, and the twins sprawled out on the carpet in front of the huge TV. I popped in the DVD and sat beside Josh on the couch, leaving space between us. Even though he appeared to be in a better place emotionally, I was still a little gun-shy around him. I'd seen his mood change too quickly lately.

Quinn and Alex giggled as WALL-E dug through a massive pile of garbage, and Josh turned up the volume on the remote before he shifted to face me.

"I'm so sorry I've been taking out my frustrations on you. You didn't deserve any of that," he said.

"I just wanted to be there for you and to help you."

"You did. You made me see I couldn't do it by myself."

"So you've been happy with the doctor?"

He nodded. "Yoga has really made a difference, and so has getting a good night's sleep."

"Have you been working on the piano lessons?"

"I've been trying, but I keep getting stuck and frustrated with it. I don't know why it's not coming back to me yet..." The familiar tightness in his face returned.

"Don't push it." I put my hand on his arm. "It sounds like you're on the right path, so just take your time."

He stared at my hand, and I worried "distant Josh" would reappear. I started to pull away, but he covered my hand with his and lifted his eyes to mine.

"I won't push, and I won't push you away again."

He held my gaze, and I saw the look in his eyes I'd yearned to see. The look that said, *I want to kiss you so badly.* I wet my lips and leaned into him, and he bent his head toward mine.

The twins howled with squeaky laughter, and Josh and I both halted, remembering we had company.

I sighed. "Guess we should watch the movie."

Josh glanced at my mouth with longing, and I debated whether we could get away with making out without the twins noticing. They *were* glued to the TV...

Josh slowly sat back, ending my debate, and I turned my attention to the movie. While WALL-E fell in love with EVE, I sank deeper into the sofa, and the week of taking care of the twins caught up to me. I didn't realize I had dozed off until I woke up to Quinn and Alex pointing and giggling and Josh smiling at me.

I raised my head. "Is the movie over?"

"Can we watch *Toy Story* now?" Alex asked.

I looked at the clock on the cable box. "It's time for bed."

He and Quinn whined and started a chorus of pleas.

"I let you stay up late last night when I shouldn't have," I said.

"Need some help getting them ready for bed?" Josh asked.

I was about to take him up on his offer, but Quinn and Alex would never go to sleep as long Josh was there. I had to sacrifice more time with him for less commotion with the twins.

"I think it's best if I do it on my own. Your irresistible charm will keep the kids up." I smiled.

He chuckled and stretched his arms as he stood. Quinn and Alex jumped down and latched on to his legs.

"Bye, Josh," they said in eerily perfect twin tandem.

He ruffled their blond heads. "I'll see you again very soon."

When I finally pried them away from him, I walked him to the door. Before I could say anything, he wrapped me in a hug, holding me longer than he had in the past three weeks combined. I pressed my face to his neck and breathed in his familiar sweet scent.

"Can you come over tomorrow?" he asked as he pulled back.

Happy dancing ensued inside me. It felt so wonderful to be invited. To be *wanted*.

"Yeah, I'm not working, so I can come by in the evening."

"Be ready to work up a sweat."

I lifted one eyebrow. "You're not going to crank up the heater on me, are you? You know my issues with hot yoga."

He laughed. "I promise I won't. But... I can't guarantee it won't get hot in there."

He gave me the same delicious smile as earlier, and he lowered his head down to mine, placing the softest of kisses on my lips. My toes curled into the rug. *More, more, more* was all I could think.

"See you tomorrow," he said.

I watched him walk to his car, and I reluctantly went back inside. Quinn and Alex were jumping on the sofa, but I was too happy to give them a good lecture. Could things finally be getting back to normal? For real?

****

Josh answered my knock on his door, and the first thing I noticed was the lack of a smile. He had his phone to his ear, and he paced into the living room as I shut the door behind me.

"I understand, Mrs. Bates, but I have a set plan for Charlie and—"

I put down my yoga mat and my duffel bag, and I leaned against the kitchen counter to watch Josh. Lines of tension marked his forehead. The relaxed version of him I'd seen the previous night was gone.

"I can't give you a definite date, but I'm trying my best—"

The conversation with one of his students' moms was obviously not going well. He couldn't even finish a sentence without being interrupted.

"I'm sorry you feel you have to do that. Charlie was making great progress with me."

The call lasted only a minute longer, and Josh tossed the phone onto the couch. "Just lost one of my students. Charlie's mom doesn't want to wait until I start teaching again. I guess I can't blame her. Who knows how long it'll be before I can freaking remember how to play."

"Maybe you can talk to her once you're giving lessons

again. Try to get her to switch him back."

"He probably won't be the only one I lose. I'm surprised the others haven't left yet."

I stayed quiet as I knew nothing I said would help. We'd been doing this same song-and-dance for weeks.

Josh rubbed the back of his neck. "I'm sorry. I didn't ask you here to listen to my issues."

"I don't want you to feel like you can't talk to me. I just want to help you get to a better place."

He came over and stood in front of me. "You are. And I'm trying to get there. Some days are just better than others."

I reached up and touched his cheek, and he tugged lightly on the strings of my hoodie.

"I did get some good news today," he said. "Ronnie said I can bus tables until I can play again, so I won't have to survive on cereal and ramen noodles."

"That's awesome. It'll be great to have you back there."

"I think it'll be good to have something to occupy me. Less time to sit around stressing out about things."

"And you'll be back on the ice Tuesday, so you'll have even less down time."

He avoided my gaze and said, "Yeah," sounding nowhere near as excited as I'd thought he'd be.

"We should umm… we should get started." He pointed his thumb at the TV. He'd already hooked up his laptop to it.

He rolled out his mat in the small space between the TV and the couch, and he pulled his T-shirt over his head. I stopped while flattening my mat.

"I thought we weren't doing hot yoga," I said.

"We're not. I can move better without the shirt." A hint of a grin curled his lips, and he patted his ripped stomach. "Is this too distracting for you?"

Distracting? I thought as I happily became visually reacquainted with his chiseled abs. More like, *How I am going to keep my hands off you?*

"Not at all," I said coolly, kicking off my sneakers and removing my hoodie. "Is this distracting for *you*?"

His grin spread to his eyes, which slowly took in my sports bra and fitted yoga pants. Goosebumps prickled the back of my neck.

"I'm good," he mimicked my cool delivery, but the lingering look he gave me said he totally wasn't.

I tightened my ponytail and did a few light stretches as Josh pulled up the video online. When the instructor began her warm-up directions, I closed my eyes and focused only on her soothing voice. I could see why Josh liked that particular video. The instructor had the most calming voice I'd ever heard.

For the next hour I was completely in the zen zone, working my body into positions I never expected to feel good. It had been a long time since I'd done yoga, but I'd have to consider adding it to my workout regimen. During a few of the transitions, Josh and I almost touched since we were in such a small space, but I made sure to keep just out of reach. I didn't want to risk knocking Josh out of his zone. Any physical contact with him and all his hotness would definitely take me out of mine.

As we completed our final cool down position, sitting cross-legged with our hands folded near our hearts, I closed my eyes once again and inhaled the peaceful energy surrounding me. Josh and I continued to sit quietly until I heard him moving next to me. I opened my eyes and found him looking at me with the smile I'd expected at the door.

"Did you enjoy it?" he asked.

"Very much. I feel almost… weightless now."

He stood and offered his hand, and I took it. Standing eye-level to his glistening chest really made me feel like I was floating… on a bubble of desire that was about to burst. But I wasn't going to make the first move. I had to let him come to me when he was ready. As torturous as it was to wait.

"Are you hungry?" he asked. "I usually make a smoothie after I finish."

I was hungry alright. *Starving.* But not for food.

"That sounds good."

Josh assembled the ingredients for the strawberry banana smoothies, and I took out a knife to slice the fruit. I started cutting, and he loaded the ice cubes into the blender and stole two strawberry slices from me.

"Hey." I swatted his hand.

He smiled devilishly as he chewed, and he watched me with growing intensity. I quickly went back to cutting to busy my hands. Otherwise, who knew where they would end up.

Josh moved behind me in the tiny kitchen, and I thought he was going to the fridge, but he stopped. So close his body heat mixed with mine. I sliced through a strawberry but froze when Josh's hand closed around my hip. He squeezed gently and slid his fingers around to my stomach. They grazed my bare skin, and I drew in a breath.

His lips left a hot path from my shoulder to my neck, and I dropped the knife and leaned back into him, needing all the support for my weightless body. He nipped at my earlobe and snaked his arm all the way around my waist.

"I need you," he said low against my ear.

The bubble exploded.

I whirled around and tackled his mouth with mine, unleashing a month's worth of frustration and anticipation. His hands framed my face and then combed into my hair, pulling my ponytail loose. I kissed his lips, his neck, his chest... everywhere I could reach. His mouth tasted strawberry sweet, while his skin was salty with sweat.

He pressed me against the fridge, and the cool steel hit my back. But Josh's lips and hands were all over me, keeping me on fire. He lifted me up, and I locked my arms around his shoulders and my legs around his waist. As he carried me into the bedroom, we dove into another deep kiss, not breaking apart until we fell onto the bed. Josh pushed up on his hands and stared down at me, and I feared he was going to pull away from me again.

But he didn't.

And for the first time in weeks, everything felt so right and *so* good. Better than good.

Perfect.

****

I slowly opened my eyes and reached out in the darkness, expecting to feel Josh's warm body beside me, but my hand landed on a vacant pillow. I sat up and saw a faint glow of light shining in the living room. Why hadn't Josh stayed with me? We hadn't been that close, that connected in so long. I wanted to hold onto it as hard I could.

I slipped out from under the blanket with a shiver and grabbed one of Josh's sweaters that was thrown over the chair. It fit me like a dress and was cozy and warm. I padded to the doorway but didn't go any farther.

Josh sat at his keyboard, wearing headphones and studying the keys. He pressed one and then another and then two at a time, all the while shaking his head. Over and over he tried key after key until he tore the headphones from his ears and bent forward, gripping his head in his hands.

I didn't hesitate to go to him as I had been doing. I went over to the bench and sat with him, speaking only with a soft kiss on his shoulder.

"I was feeling so good that I thought I might remember." He stared achingly at the keyboard. "I wanted to surprise you and play for you..."

I put my arm around him and massaged his neck, trying to keep the tension from overtaking him again. He looked up at me, his eyes cloudy with sadness.

"When am I going to be me again?"

I broke apart at the despair in his voice. I had to make him realize how far he'd come already. I'd felt it when I had been in his arms.

"You're still you." I placed my hand over his heart. "In here. That's never changed."

"Just like tonight you were finally able to show your passion and your love for me, you'll be able to do that with your music soon… and your skating. I know it."

He rested his forehead against mine, and I threaded my fingers into his hair, slowly caressing his dark locks.

"Come here," he whispered.

He pulled me onto his lap, and I straddled his thighs. Our faces were just an inch apart, and his loving gaze sent warm shivers through me. He brushed his thumb across my cheek and along my jaw, and I wound my arms around him.

"I would be so lost without you," he said, looking deep into my eyes.

I leaned in and kissed him gently at first, then more intently, proving to him the words I was about to speak.

"I'll always be here."

Chapter Eight

The loud hum of the Zamboni circling the ice drowned out my training mates' chit-chat, which was fine with me. Something more important required my attention — Josh lacing up his skates beside me. He'd given only tense smiles to everyone who had welcomed him back for his first on-ice training day. I'd asked him over the weekend if he felt ready to skate again, and he'd said yes but had quickly changed the subject.

I secured the knots on my own laces and pulled my green leg warmers down over them. I'd woken up an hour early that morning, so anxious to skate with Josh again. We wouldn't be doing any more than simple stroking, but I was so excited just to hold Josh's hand on the ice. Skating solo the past month had made me feel beyond lonely.

Sergei came down from the lounge with two large cups of coffee, and he handed one to Em. "This is the biggest cup I could find."

"Thank you, Love." She turned to Josh and me. "This is my fifth already. I should just hook myself up to a coffee IV."

"Jet lag from hell?" I asked.

"My body thinks it's bedtime right now." She took a long sip of her drink. "Josh, if I fall asleep on the ice, don't take it personally. I really am so thrilled to have you back today."

He didn't look nearly as thrilled. He rose from the bleachers and stood at the boards, watching the Zamboni exit the ice. I went to his side and followed his eyes as they darted around the rink.

"It's totally understandable if you're nervous about getting back out there," I said.

He tapped his hands rhythmically on the boards. "I just need to get started."

He headed for the ice door and removed his skate guards, but he waited for the other pairs on our session to hop through the door first. I brought up the rear and took off across the ice to warm up. Josh would be doing light stroking on his own to start, so I needed to give him space. Hovering near him would probably just make him jumpier.

I peeked behind me as I rounded the corner. Josh had finally stepped onto the ice. The rest of us were motoring around at high speed, but he was gliding slowly as he hung out near the boards. It was strange to see him so tentative when he usually blew past everyone.

"The Resistance" streamed through the sound system, and I smiled at Em as she turned up the volume. Muse was one of Josh's favorite bands. I tried to catch his eye, but he had his head down, zoned into the ice.

I picked up my pace and leaned on deeper edges as I went around and around the rink. Josh had started to move a little faster, too, and my heart smiled at the sight of him looking more at ease. I loved watching him skate. He had such a natural connection with the ice.

As I passed him, I reached out and brushed his arm, and he jumped and jerked away. I quickly recoiled, too.

"Sorry," we both said.

"I didn't know it was you," he said, while I spoke at the

same time, "I shouldn't have—"

"I was just concentrating," he said.

I nodded. "You're doing great."

Don't crowd him. Let him do his thing.

I left him and resumed my warm-up, keeping one eye trained on him. As the minutes ticked by, Josh drifted farther away from the boards, and his posture straightened even more. I moved with added zip in my step as I sensed his confidence was slowly returning.

When our mid-morning break came, Josh blew out a long breath and accepted warm pats on the back from Em and Sergei. He and I brought our protein bars up to the lounge and sat at one of the small tables near the glass wall.

"You must be relieved to have that first step done," I said.

"My legs were so shaky when I started," he said. "But I finally got a good feel for the ice."

His phone buzzed, and he clicked on it to read the text. "It's from Steph."

I glanced at the big clock above the rink. Stephanie must have had a morning class at fashion design school if she was up that early on the West Coast.

"I talked to her last night." Josh set aside the phone. "They're all coming here for Christmas."

"All?" I looked at him over the rim of my water bottle. "As in Stephanie and your parents?"

"I was as surprised as you are. Then Steph told me they're going to some big party a few days later in New York City, so it all made sense. They're just stopping here on the way."

"Where are they staying?"

"At a hotel in Boston."

I fiddled with my ponytail. "Can we visit with them separately on Christmas? I really don't want to invite them to my parents' house. They're just going to make everything uncomfortable and be all judgmental about where my parents live."

"That's fine with me."

I crumpled my protein bar wrapper and squeezed it in my fist. I'd thought we would have a relaxing holiday — dinner with Mrs. Cassar on Christmas Eve and then a quiet celebration with my parents the next day. Josh was still working through his anxiety, and having his family in town would no doubt lead to more agitation.

We returned to the ice a few minutes later, and Sergei stopped me before I could take off on my own.

"Ready to skate with your partner?" He grinned.

I jumped up and down with glee on the inside but kept my giddiness in check on the outside. Sergei instructed us to do crossovers together, one of the basic exercises we had done when we'd first teamed up. Josh took my hand, and he held it so fiercely I thought he might crush the bones in my fingers.

"I know you got me." I smiled.

He loosened his grip a bit, and we began to push across the ice with identical strokes. Soon we were circling the rink with sweeping crossovers. Em motioned a few times for us to slow down, but it was hard not to get overly excited and fly faster. Having Josh beside me made me feel like a complete skater.

Just doing the easy warm-up exercise with Josh also had my competitive juices flowing again. We had six weeks until nationals, and I wanted so badly to be on the ice in Greensboro, to perform the beautiful programs we'd poured our hearts into perfecting. I couldn't get ahead of myself, though. We had a lot of training time to make up, and Josh had only taken baby steps so far.

He turned his head and made eye contact with me, and his bright smile strengthened our belief in us. It gave me renewed hope we could conquer all the challenges ahead. One stroke at a time.

****

I opened my locker and bounced on my heels. A new gift from my Secret Santa awaited me. I grabbed the small gift bag and carried it out to the rink. For the past week, Santa had given me a variety of presents — from a strawberry-scented candle to a pair of furry green earmuffs. I pulled the tissue paper from the bag and found a figurine of Donald and Daisy Duck as a figure skating pair.

Josh saw my wide smile, and he grinned just as big. "What you got there? Is that from your Secret Santa?"

"I wonder who that person could be..." I tapped my chin and gave him a knowing look.

"You'll find out very soon." His eyebrows danced.

With holiday music playing on the stereo and our rink party later that day, everyone was in a festive mood. Only a few days remained before Christmas. On the ice, Josh and I had advanced from simple stroking to doing spins and double jumps. We had also practiced all our lifts off the ice. Em and Sergei had a steady plan for us as we inched closer to nationals.

I stashed my gift in the locker room and hustled back to the ice for the start of the next session. Josh was already out there, waiting for our next task from Em and Sergei.

"You're one minute late." He tugged on my ponytail and smiled. "Slacker."

"It's time to put the lifts on the ice," Sergei said.

Josh's smile vanished. "Already?"

"You're right on schedule with where we hoped you'd be. It's the next step toward doing sections of your programs."

"You're ready," Em said. "We wouldn't ask you to do this if you weren't."

I grasped Josh's hand and looked up at him. "Our timing with them on the floor has been great. We got this."

He shuffled his skates and remained quiet as Sergei

directed us to do the star lift first. We set off from the boards, and Josh's hold on my hand intensified.

"Just like riding a bike," I said, trying to maintain the positive mood.

I wasn't sure Josh had even heard me. He was staring down at the ice and didn't give me any kind of response. I was going to have to kick us into action to get his attention.

"Ready?" I said and sped up my skates.

Josh had no choice but to follow me or be dragged behind. We transitioned into matching crossovers and gathered more speed, and we moved into position for the lift entry. I put my hand on Josh's shoulder while he set his on my hip, and I waited for him to press me into the air.

And waited… and waited…

Josh's chest puffed in and out in quick spurts, and a sheen of sweat covered his forehead. I reached up to touch his flushed cheek, but he dashed past me and grabbed onto the boards, facing away from the ice. I called his name and raced over to him.

He bent his head, and his hands shook as he braced them on the boards. He was still breathing rapidly.

What's happening? Is he having a panic attack?

I rubbed up and down his spine. "Try to take deep breaths."

He closed his eyes and slowly inhaled and exhaled. I kept massaging his back, and I gave Em and Sergei a wide-eyed look as they skated over to us.

"Josh, what's wrong?" Em asked.

"I'm okay," he whispered, but his head remained down.

"Let's go sit." Em gently took his elbow.

He carefully lifted his head and glided between Em and Sergei to the ice door. I followed, and we all sat on the bleachers.

"What happened?" Sergei asked.

Josh drank from his water bottle and wiped his glistening

face with a towel. "My heart started beating really fast, and I couldn't catch my breath."

"Have you felt that way any other time since you've been back on the ice?" Em asked.

"No, it was just… just right now."

When we were about to do a lift for the first time since the accident.

"Maybe we should take you to the ER to make sure you're okay," Em said.

"I'm fine. I feel fine now," Josh insisted.

"I had a panic attack once," I said. "I felt the same way… like I couldn't breathe. I almost passed out."

Em put her hand on Josh's arm. "You don't have to be nervous. You've trained these lifts for so long. Trust in that training."

Josh didn't say anything, and Sergei asked, "Do you want to try doing it again?"

Josh stared at the ice for a long minute, and he only gave a quiet nod in reply. We returned to the ice, and I stood in front of him so he'd have to look at me.

"Hey," I said softly and grasped his waist. "I trust you. Completely."

He held my gaze momentarily and then took one of my hands. With a quick push of his blades, he urged us across the ice. I followed his lead and tracked my steps with his.

As we did crossovers around the rink, Josh's grip on my hand became clammy, and I watched him closely. He was visibly breathing hard again. He squeezed my hand tighter, and the shakiness of his arm vibrated mine. He was not okay.

I started to say his name, but he let go of me before I could finish. He turned and hunched forward with his hands on his thighs. I had visions of him passing out right there on the ice.

I put my arm around him and quickly steered him to the boards, away from the skater traffic. He bent all the way forward so his elbows rested on the wooden barrier.

"We don't have to do this now." I smoothed my palm along the back of his T-shirt.

Em began to move toward us, but I signaled for her to give us space. The other pairs gave us concerned looks as they continued their training around us.

When Josh eventually stood tall, I saw how sweat-soaked his face was. He looked as if he had done an entire program run-through.

"I'm sorry," he said.

"There's nothing to be sorry for. You're doing the best you can."

"I should be able to do better. I *want* to do better. I just can't…" He clenched his fingers in his hair. "I keep feeling the sensation of my feet slipping and you falling."

"That was a fluke thing. You've done thousands of lifts perfectly."

"I know, but all I can see is that one. That horrible one."

The pain of the memory showed in his eyes, and I didn't know how to erase it. All I could do was remind him he could lean on me anytime he needed. I wrapped him in a long hug and listened to his heartbeat slowly return to normal.

"Maybe you should talk to the psychologist about this," I said.

"I doubt I can get in with her during the holidays." He pulled back a little so he faced me. "And we don't have time to wait for whenever I can see her. I have to do this myself. I have to keep trying to get past this."

How was he going to do that? By giving himself panic attacks until they hopefully stopped? I couldn't stand seeing him in that state. But I had no idea how to help him trust himself again.

Chapter Nine

We'd tried everything.

We'd practiced the lift entrances without Josh picking me up. We'd done the lifts while stationary on the ice. We'd watched our training videos from the summer.

Nothing had worked.

Every time we tried to actually execute a lift, Josh backed off. He had a mental block he seemingly couldn't overcome.

The past few days had raised Josh's frustration level again as he fought his internal struggle. While working through our Christmas Eve morning practice, we made another attempt at the press lift, the most basic overhead one in skating. Josh and I clasped hands, but as soon as the moment came to press me into the air, he dropped my hands and sped off the ice. I zoomed along the same path and caught up to him as he snapped on his skate guards.

"Josh, don't—"

"Why can't I do this?" he growled at himself.

I touched his arm. "We'll just keep trying and—"

"I have to take a break. This is making me crazy."

He stormed toward the locker room, running into a trash

can and kicking it aside. I was so busy watching him I didn't notice Stephanie until she marched up to me.

"What did you do?" she snapped. "Josh never acts like that."

I am SO not in the mood for this.

"What are you doing here?" I barked. "I thought you'd be sleeping after taking the red-eye."

"I asked our driver to bring me down so I could see Josh." She folded her arms over her sleek leather coat. "Since you're hogging him until tomorrow night."

I slapped on my skate guards. "Now isn't a good time."

"I'm going to talk to my brother." She started for the locker room.

"Don't," I yelled after her and then calmed my voice, "Please let him be. He needs a few minutes alone."

"What's going on?"

I sighed and massaged my temples. I couldn't keep the truth from her. She was going to find out eventually, especially if Josh and I had to pull out of nationals... which was looking more likely each day we couldn't run our full programs.

"Josh hasn't been able to do any of the lifts. He can't get past what happened at Skate America."

She stared at me like she couldn't process what I'd said. "He's never been scared of anything on the ice."

"The accident really shook him. It's affected him more than just physically."

"He's sounded fine when I've talked to him. He never said there were any problems from the concussion."

"He didn't want you to know he's had a rough time. He thought he'd be fine by the time you visited, but he's not." I picked up my water bottle and twiddled with the cap. "He's had a lot of anxiety and... he hasn't been able to play the piano like he used to."

She gaped at me. "He forgot how to play?"

I nodded slowly. "It's been incredibly hard for him."

"What do the doctors say? I mean, he's going to remember, right?"

"He's working on it, but it's taking some time."

"How could he not tell me about this?" She narrowed her blue eyes. "Did you make him lie to me?"

Of course she would automatically place the blame on me.

"Steph?" Josh emerged from the locker room.

Stephanie rushed over and strangled him in a hug. "You should've told me you were so messed up."

Josh looked at me over her shoulder, and I gave him my best apologetic face.

"Is your doctor not helping you?" Stephanie rolled on. "I'm sure Dad can find a better one in Boston."

"My doctor's helped me a lot."

"Well, obviously not enough or you wouldn't be kicking trash cans."

Josh rubbed his forehead. "It's been a rough few days."

"From what Courtney said, it sounds like it's been more than a few days." Stephanie grew louder. "Josh, music and skating are your life. You can't lose those things."

I winced as that awful possibility paled Josh's face. He didn't need Stephanie's panicky drama freaking him out.

"I'm not going to lose them," he said quietly.

Stephanie's mouth stopped running for a minute, and she stood completely still, looking at Josh with concern. When she finally moved, she embraced him again. Just like when we'd been at the hospital, I could see how much Stephanie genuinely cared for Josh. Even if she didn't always choose the best way to show it.

Josh slowly peeled himself from Stephanie's arms and turned to me. "We should get back to practice. Everything but the lifts."

"Yeah, let's do it."

"Are you gonna hang out a while?" Josh asked Stephanie.

"I was going to, but Dad called on my way down and he wants the car back sooner. I can only stay a few minutes."

"We can talk more tomorrow night," Josh said.

Stephanie took a seat on the bleachers, and Josh and I prepared to take the ice again. I stopped him as we reached the boards.

"I'm sorry I spilled everything to her," I said. "She caught me at a bad moment."

"It's okay. I wouldn't have been able to pretend everything is fine for long. It's much easier to do two thousand miles away."

He took my hand, and we skated over to Em and Sergei. They gave us a new plan for the rest of the session, and we quickly got back to work.

Stephanie watched us intently from the sideline, and I wondered what she was going to say to her parents about Josh's condition. No doubt she would tell them the news. The only question was how they were going to use that information to make our Christmas dinner even more unpleasant.

****

"I can't believe Mrs. Cassar gave us such expensive gifts when she's already given us so much," I said as I led Josh into Em and Sergei's kitchen.

"My leather jacket must've cost a couple hundred dollars," Josh said.

I held up my large gift bag. "I know this Kate Spade purse and wallet sure did."

In addition to the presents, Mrs. Cassar had also insisted on paying for our Christmas Eve dinner. For an elderly woman, she had the reflexes of a teenager. She'd snatched the bill before Josh and I could put up any money.

After taking off my coat, I turned on the TV and tuned to the holiday music channel. Em, Sergei, and the twins had gone to Boston for dinner with Em's family, so they wouldn't be home for a while. I plugged in the huge Christmas tree and switched off the living room lamps, so only the tiny white lights lit up the room.

Josh set his duffel bag beside the tree. "It was really great of Em to invite me to stay here tonight... even if I have to sleep in Liza's room."

He pinched my waist, and I smiled. Liza was with her mom in New York, so her bed was conveniently available.

I linked my arm through Josh's. "Em just doesn't want the twins to see us staying in the same room."

"Won't they be asleep with visions of sugar plums in their heads?"

I laughed and stepped out of my high heels. "Knowing Quinn, she'll talk Alex into trying to sneak a peek at Santa. Sergei better be super stealth down here when he's eating the cookies and milk."

We sat on the couch, and I pointed at the mantle above the fireplace. "Did you notice the newest stocking?"

Josh's eyes fell upon the red one monogrammed with a gold "J." His face beamed with a huge grin. "That's for me?"

"You're part of the family."

He snuggled me closer to him and rested his cheek against the top of my head. "It's funny how people I've known a year and a half feel more like family than the people I'm actually related to."

I tilted my neck to look up at him. "Em and Sergei care so much about you, and you know the twins freaking adore you."

"What about you?" He tapped the tip of my nose. "How do you feel about me?"

I shrugged. "You're alright, I guess."

"*Alright?*" He tickled my side.

I yelped. "I think you need to remind me of my true feelings."

"Is that so? Well, let's see if this helps."

His fingers curled behind my neck and into my hair, raising goose bumps down my spine. He leaned slowly into me, his eyes on mine, and he brushed my lips with a kiss.

"Mmmm... it's starting to come back to me," I said.

He lowered his mouth to the curve of my neck, and his hot breath on my skin made me tingle everywhere. I grabbed his tie and clenched it as he kissed his way north to my ear.

"You still think I'm just alright?" he asked huskily.

I shivered and shook my head. His mouth met mine once again, and my heart cried out with all the feelings I had for him. They were so many and so powerful I could never put them into words.

We separated for a momentary breath, and I pressed Josh's hand to my chest. "Do you feel this? This is what I think of you... what I feel for you. Every crazy fast beat of my heart... all for you."

I lifted my hand, but Josh kept his over the rapid pounding. He inched down the neckline of my dress and bent his head, touching his lips to my breastbone. My pulse flew into a full sprint.

Lost in a flurry of hot kisses and whispered declarations of love, I forgot where we were until the phone rang and Em's answering machine greeting picked up. Her voice reminded me we wouldn't be alone that night.

I reluctantly broke away from Josh's lips. "As much as I'd love to continue this, we should probably cool down."

He groaned and tipped our foreheads together. "I'm going to be thinking about you all night."

"I'll be the sugar plum dancing in your head?" I giggled.

His mouth crooked into a smile, and he ran his finger lightly down my arm. "Something like that."

"Why don't we exchange gifts? That'll be a good

distraction."

"I thought you were opposed to opening gifts on Christmas Eve."

I slipped out of his embrace and knelt in front of the tree. "We can start a new tradition. It'll be too chaotic tomorrow morning with the twins and all their loot."

Josh went over to his duffel and pulled out a tiny box wrapped in shiny green paper. I shifted a few presents under the tree and plucked Josh's two gifts from the mountainous pile.

"You have two for me?" he said. "I only have one for you."

"You gave me all those Secret Santa gifts, which I loved. They were all so thoughtful." I kissed him as he sat beside me. "Here, open one of yours first."

I gave him the smaller box, and he removed the wrapping with one tear. He peered curiously at the leather cuff bracelet.

"I know you've never worn anything like it, but my mom was making them, and I thought it would look really good on you, so we designed this one together," I said.

"Your mom made this?" He fingered the black braided leather. "That's really cool."

He unbuttoned the sleeve of his dress shirt and rolled up the cuff so he could snap the bracelet around his wrist. It fit almost perfectly over his sinewy muscles.

"It looks hotter than I imagined," I said, caressing the soft hair on his forearm.

"I'm sold on it, then." He grinned.

I pictured how good the bracelet would look on his arm as he played the piano — an added edge to his already sexy hands. But I couldn't voice that to him. I didn't want him to know how much I missed watching him play.

He thanked me with a long kiss and presented me with my gift. "Your turn."

I made a big production of examining the box from all sides before delicately tearing the paper. It was too pretty to destroy. I peeked up at Josh watching me with anticipation, and I opened the black velvet box, revealing a stunning pair of emerald stud earrings.

"Josh." I gasped. "They're gorgeous."

"I wanted to find something to match your eyes." He swept a long curl from my cheek. "But it wasn't easy since your eyes are so beautiful."

I smiled and skimmed the shimmering stones with my finger. "They're exquisite. You didn't have to spend this much on me, though."

"I wanted to. As soon as I saw them, I knew they were meant for you."

I quickly removed the dangly earrings I was wearing and slipped the studs into place. "How do they look?"

His admiring gaze warmed me deep in my core. "Perfect."

I leaned forward and kissed him, and his silky lips returned my thanks and then some. I eventually sat back and picked up Josh's remaining present, but I hesitated with it in my lap. I'd gotten it months ago and had debated whether I should wait to give it to him. The last thing I wanted was to make him sad on Christmas.

"Is that mine?" he asked with a smile.

I slowly handed it to him. "I hope… I hope you like it."

He opened the flat box carefully, and his eyes doubled in size when he saw what was inside — the sheet music for "Exogenesis Symphony Part 3," autographed by all the members of Muse. It was one of our special songs — one Josh played for me all the time. Back when he could…

"How did you—" Josh's voice stuck. "Where did you get this?"

"Em's agent knows a guy who knows a guy, and he got it for me when the band had their show in L.A."

He remained mesmerized, tracing the signatures scrawled on the cover. "This is so awesome. I'm gonna frame it and hang it above my keyboard."

I let out a breath of relief, but then the light in Josh's eyes dimmed as he flipped through the pages.

"I wish I could play it for you," he said.

My chest tightened. That was where I'd been afraid his mind would go.

"I can wait." I squeezed his hand.

He set the music down and wrapped me in his arms. "You've had to do a lot of waiting for me."

And I would do so much more.

"Hey," I said softly and faced him. "I know how badly you want to play for me and to fully skate with me. I want you to be able to do those things, too, because they mean so much to you. But all I need from you is what you've never stopped giving me — your love."

Josh swallowed hard, and he brought me tight against his body. His lips buried tiny kisses in my hair.

"That will never stop."

Chapter Ten

I'd expected the Taj Hotel in Boston to be super fancy from its name, but it managed to exceed my expectations. The marble floor in the lobby looked as if it was polished every hour, and the decor screamed "antique." The Tuckers knew how to travel in style — I'd give them that much.

"Steph just texted me," Josh said and read aloud, "'Mom wants to eat in the suite, so she ordered room service for us.'"

"She probably doesn't want to be seen with me in the restaurant," I said.

Josh pushed the elevator button and joined our hands. "If she starts giving you a hard time, we're out the door."

"Then we should probably keep our coats on."

We stepped into the elevator, and I took off my knit hat and combed my frazzled curls with my fingers. No matter how much I told myself I shouldn't care what Mrs. Tucker thought of me, I always felt self-conscious in her presence. I was especially antsy because I'd be seeing Josh's dad for only the second time. Our first conversation hadn't exactly been a heartwarming chat.

Josh knocked on the room door, and Stephanie answered.

While she tackled him with one of her many hugs as of late, I walked inside and took in the luxuriousness of the suite. There was a sitting area, a full-sized dining table, and even a fireplace. I'd only seen a hotel room like that on TV.

Mrs. Tucker rose from the gold-colored couch. She wore a fuzzy white sweater and black leather pants, and her solid diamond necklace blinded me from across the room.

"Hello," she said.

Hello? Even the sales clerk at the gas station that morning had greeted me with "Merry Christmas." I shifted the bag of gifts I was holding from one hand to the other and put on my cheeriest smile.

"Merry Christmas," I said.

Her expression remained cool, and she gave me one of her critical once-overs on her way to welcoming Josh. Meanwhile, Mr. Tucker emerged from what I assumed was the bedroom.

"Hello, Courtney," he said.

Are these people not aware it's a holiday?

"Merry Christmas," I said even louder than before.

"Let me take your coat," he said. "What can I get you to drink?"

Mr. Tucker draped my pea coat over one of the formal chairs in the sitting area, and I eyed the bottle of Scotch on the dining table. A shot of hard liquor could make the evening more tolerable. It would also probably make me say some things I shouldn't.

"Umm... diet soda, please."

Mr. Tucker went to the table and poured my soda over ice. "Regular for you, Son?"

Josh stared at the Scotch and the bottle of wine beside it. Even though he'd never had a drink in his life, he was probably having the same thought I'd had.

He lifted his eyes to his dad. "Yeah, thanks."

"I had a migraine earlier, so I didn't feel like sitting in a noisy restaurant," Mrs. Tucker said. "Catering brought up some food for us."

On the table were a vegetable platter, a cheese and fruit assortment, and some kind of hors d'oeuvre I couldn't identify. That had to be cocktail food, right? It surely couldn't be our meal.

"Are we ordering dinner?" Josh read my mind.

"We had a late lunch, so this is all we need," Mrs. Tucker said as she sat on the couch.

I sipped my drink and picked up a celery stick. *Well, I don't have to worry about putting on any holiday weight.*

"Are these for us?" Stephanie poked into the bag we'd brought.

"They're from Court and me," Josh said.

"Yours are next to the fireplace." Mrs. Tucker pointed him to the perfectly-wrapped gifts on the marble hearth.

He picked up the two boxes and looked at all eight sides. "Which is mine and which is Court's?"

"They're both yours," Mrs. Tucker said.

Josh's mouth hung open. "You didn't get Court a gift?"

"I didn't know what she likes."

"And you couldn't pick up the phone and ask me?"

Heat spread from my cheeks down to my neck, and I ducked my head. I shouldn't have been surprised Mrs. Tucker would snub me that way. She thrived on making me feel excluded. I wasn't going to give her the satisfaction of seeing my disappointment, though.

"It's okay," I said quietly.

"No, it's not." Josh put his presents on the coffee table. "You can keep these. I don't want them."

Mrs. Tucker pursed her lips. "Josh, you're being rude."

"*I'm* being rude?"

Mr. Tucker came over with his Scotch. "We can open the gifts later. Courtney, I apologize for the oversight."

Josh let out a dry laugh and muttered, "Oversight."

I sat on the chair that held my coat and gripped my glass with both my sweaty palms. The uncomfortable edge in the room had me shaking inside.

I might be the one having a panic attack tonight.

"How's your training for nationals going?" Mr. Tucker asked. "Did you lose much time after the accident?"

Josh and I both looked at Stephanie. She hadn't run and told everything she'd learned at the rink?

"I thought I'd let you tell Mom and Dad what's been going on," Stephanie said to Josh's shocked face.

"Is there a problem?" Mr. Tucker asked.

Josh lowered his head and stared at his drink. He didn't like talking about his issues, and having to explain them in the already tense environment had to be a total nightmare for him.

"Josh?" his dad pressed.

"I can't do the lifts. It's... it's a mental thing."

Mr. Tucker's brow wrinkled. "What do you mean you can't do them?"

"I mean my brain won't allow my body to physically do them," Josh said in a strained voice.

I reached up to where he stood beside my chair and I touched his arm. I could feel the agitation radiating from him. He would rather walk through hot coals than admit any kind of defeat to his parents.

"So, you probably won't be competing at nationals," Mr. Tucker said.

"I think this is happening for a reason," Mrs. Tucker said. "It's a sign you're supposed to leave skating behind and move on with your life."

Oh my God, she just won't let it go.

"He can't play the piano either," Stephanie said. "What's that a sign for?"

I did a double-take at Stephanie sassing her mother. Was she really on our side?

Mr. Tucker's phone rang, and he didn't hesitate to

answer, "Merry Christmas, Paul."

I guess it's just me who doesn't warrant a holiday greeting.

He moved into the dining area, and he laughed in the background as the rest of us observed each other, waiting for the next sharp comment. My money was on Stephanie to deliver.

"Mom, did you hear me?" Stephanie proved me right. "Josh forgot how to play the piano."

Mrs. Tucker's phone dinged with an alert, and she also didn't hesitate to respond to it. Her attention remained on the phone even after she finished typing. Apparently, neither she nor Mr. Tucker thought Josh's struggles were worthy of their concern.

"Mom!" Stephanie said.

"I heard you. I'm sure he'll remember. He's been playing since he was a child." Mrs. Tucker pressed her right temple. "I feel the migraine coming back. I think I'll go lie down."

"You're leaving in the middle of this?" Stephanie's volume rose.

"Why are you being so loud?"

"I don't know. Maybe because you don't seem to care that Josh is having major psychological issues."

Josh rubbed his forehead while I downed the rest of my soda. The last thing I'd expected was an argument between Stephanie and her mother. Or Stephanie as the voice of reason.

"You're being overly dramatic, don't you think?" Mrs. Tucker said. Her phone chimed again as she carried it with her to the bedroom, and she shut the door behind her.

"Wow," I whispered against the rim of my glass. I couldn't grasp Mrs. Tucker's complete lack of emotion regarding her son's well-being. Josh had received more compassion from customers at the restaurant who only knew him as the guy who played the piano.

"Un-believable," Stephanie said.

"What is?" Mr. Tucker rejoined us.

"Mom acting like Josh is perfectly fine."

Josh's face had grown redder over the course of the conversation, and I didn't know how much longer he could endure the fiasco.

Mr. Tucker sipped his drink. "Josh, since you can't skate—"

"I can skate," he said tersely.

"But you probably won't be ready for nationals at this rate. You should take a few days off from training and come to New York with us. The party we're attending is a great chance to network and find new opportunities."

"He doesn't need a party. He needs help!" Stephanie exclaimed.

"I need air." Josh banged his glass down on the coffee table and looked at me. "Do you wanna take a walk?"

I couldn't believe I was hesitating over getting away from the very un-merry gathering, but something Stephanie had said had sparked an idea.

"You go ahead. I need to talk to Stephanie."

Her finely sculpted eyebrows rose, and Josh gave me an equally surprised look.

I stood and leaned in close to him. "I'll be fine."

He glanced at his father and Stephanie, lingering a few more moments before he kissed my forehead and left the room.

"You want to talk to *me*?" Stephanie said.

I reclaimed my seat. "Yes, about Josh."

"I have a call to make," Mr. Tucker said and returned to the dining area.

"What about him?" Stephanie asked.

"You and I don't have much in common, but we both love Josh and we agree on one important thing — he needs help. And I have an idea how you might be able to give it to him."

She tilted her head to one side. "I'm listening."

"Even though Josh and I have a great connection on the

ice, nothing can compare to all the years of experience you two have together. Specifically, years of doing lifts together."

Recognition widened her eyes. "I think I see where you're going with this."

"I've tried and tried to help him get past his mental block, and nothing's worked. But you know how he thinks and reacts on the ice better than anyone." I paused and looked directly at her. "Could you come to the rink tomorrow and work with him?"

"You want me to skate with him?"

I nodded.

Her lips twitched like she was trying to hide her smile, and she leaned slightly forward. "You must really be desperate to ask me for help."

Dammit, Stephanie, don't make me regret this.

"I realize you're not exactly our biggest cheerleader, but you know how important skating is to Josh... how much he wants to compete. And I know you want him to be able to do what makes him happy."

She sat back and gave me a long look. "I actually have my skates with me. I went to Frog Pond yesterday."

"That's perfect."

"I'm supposed to leave tomorrow morning, but I'll have my flight changed. If Josh needs me, I'll be there."

The knot in my chest loosened, and I let out a breath. "Thank you. I appreciate it more than you know."

If she was willing to help, that meant she was okay with Josh skating with me. Otherwise, she would have let us continue to struggle. She wasn't going to admit it, but I'd take actions over words if it meant getting us past our roadblock.

"I'm gonna go find Josh," I said. "Thank you again for changing your plans."

I walked out into the hallway and stopped before reaching the elevator. Had I made the right move? Stephanie was being very cooperative, but her method of helping remained to be seen. What if she went into full-on bitch mode and made Josh's situation worse? Trusting her was a huge leap, but I had to do it. All my options had run out, and soon time to prepare for nationals would, too.

****

Stephanie was waiting for us when Josh and I arrived at the rink. She'd already warmed up and was rocketing around the ice. After we stretched and put on our skates, she curved toward the boards and skidded to a stop.

"I don't get to skate much anymore, so I got here early," she said.

"I'll let you guys do your thing," I said.

I skated over to Em in the corner of the rink and looked over my shoulder. "This will either go brilliantly or be a total disaster."

"I was kinda thinking the same thing." She patted my shoulder. "But I do think it's definitely worth trying."

The music cranked up, and I took off across the ice, a strange sensation in my stomach. Seeing Josh warming up with Stephanie made me feel like we'd traveled back in time. All I was missing was my former partner Mark next to me.

Sergei had suggested Josh and Stephanie skate their last short program to hopefully trick Josh's muscle memory into completing the lift. When Em turned on their music, I was really blasted back to the past. Except I wasn't watching them with envy as I'd done when we had been rivals. I was watching with a bucket full of hope.

I hung close to the boards as Josh and Stephanie stroked in tandem through the opening section of the program. They did double jumps instead of the usual triples and then sped up for the lift. Their hands connected, and I stopped moving and held my breath.

And Josh backed down.

My shoulders dropped, and behind me Sergei muttered, "Damn."

Em restarted the music, and Stephanie and Josh marked the first few elements as if they were doing a partial run-through. As the concerto built in tempo, they again got into position for the lift, but the result was the same — Stephanie's feet didn't leave the ice.

They returned to their opening pose and tried the sequence once more, and my hope sank further with yet another unsuccessful attempt. Josh put his hands on his head and looked at the high ceiling as if he was summoning help from above. I wanted to go to him, but I had to give Stephanie more time.

As I skated past them, Stephanie took Josh's arm. "Let's go talk."

They walked to the locker room, and I wished I had supersonic hearing to know what they were saying. I went back to work and set up for a triple Salchow, but with my focus off the ice, my butt crashed onto the ice. I popped up and swept the cold debris from my pants as I made my way to the exit. Josh and Stephanie never had heart-to-heart talks, so my curiosity couldn't be contained.

I slipped my guards over my blades and crept to the partially open locker room door. Peeking inside, I saw Stephanie and Josh sitting on one of the benches. I quickly moved out of sight but stayed close to listen.

"Do you remember when we moved up to intermediate and I was freaking out about the overhead lift?" Stephanie asked.

"You kept saying, 'It's too high. What if I fall?'" Josh said.

"And you told me, 'You're not going to fall because I'll always protect you.' And you did. You always made me feel safe."

My throat burned with tears as I pictured a young Josh reassuring his little sister and giving her confidence. I'd never thought I would hear Stephanie speak so lovingly. It gave me a warm, fuzzy feeling — something totally foreign to my usual encounters with her.

"It was so easy then," Josh said. "I never doubted myself."

"The only way to get past the doubt now is to work through it. Look it straight in the eye and knock it down. That's what you told me when we were kids, remember?"

Josh was quiet, and after a long stretch of silence, Stephanie said, "Take my hand."

I tiptoed away from the door and dropped my guards on the bleachers. Josh and Stephanie came out of the locker room hand in hand and followed me onto the ice.

"This is home," Stephanie said. "There's no reason to doubt anything here."

I smiled to myself at her pep talk and watched Josh listen to her intently. They glided around the rink together at an easy pace, and when they picked up speed and whizzed past me, I locked my fingers together in prayer.

They joined both hands again for the lift, and Stephanie nodded energetically to Josh. Nothing happened. I squeezed my fingers harder.

Stephanie nodded once more and said something to Josh, and his shoulders rose with a visibly strong breath. He pressed up on Stephanie's hands, and she shot into the air, an ecstatic grin on her face. I shrieked and jumped up and down.

"Yes!"

Josh's eyes were wide as he rotated with Stephanie over his head. He was probably in shock he'd finally overcome his doubts and fears. Tears welled in my eyes as my own shock wore off and relief overwhelmed me.

Josh set Stephanie down carefully, and she leapt into his arms.

"You did it!" she shouted.

I sprinted over to them and smothered them both in a

group hug. We all trembled with the collective release of our emotions.

"I can't breathe," Stephanie said as she nudged her way out of my embrace.

"Sorry, sorry." I stepped back. "I just can't thank you enough."

Her eyes glistened as she looked at Josh, and she cleared her throat. "I'm glad I could help."

Josh hugged her to his side, and I saw her fighting to hold herself together. I had the feeling skating with Josh had been just as meaningful for her as it had been for him.

"You guys should keep going," I said. "Don't wanna mess with a good thing."

Josh pulled me into his arms, and the relief in his body warmed mine.

"I'll be here when you're ready," I said softly.

He and Stephanie talked with Em and Sergei, and they didn't waste any time getting to the star lift. Josh's feet moved slower and more cautiously than when he was at his best, but I was thrilled to see him just doing the element. The confidence and speed would come with time and practice.

While Josh and Stephanie did all the basic lifts, I flew around the ice, anxiously awaiting my turn. When they parted with a hug and Stephanie hopped through the ice door, I skated over to Josh.

"She's not leaving yet, is she? I wanted to thank her again."

"She's just getting changed. She wants to watch us skate." He saw my eyebrows rise. "I think she feels invested in us now that she's a part of our comeback."

Em circled around us while keeping an eye on another student. "Josh, do you need a break?"

"No, I wanna keep this rolling. I'm ready for what's next."

"Great." She gave us a wide smile. "Let's start simple.

Press lift first and then work your way up like you did with Stephanie."

Josh took my hand, and we did light stroking together to get our timing down. Once we'd established a good rhythm, he led me into the setup for the lift. We'd gone through those motions so many times with no success that I couldn't help but tighten with nerves. He'd had a breakthrough with Stephanie, but there was no certainty he could repeat it with me. After all, *I* had been the one on the ice with him when he'd fallen. One look at me might remind him again of that terrible moment.

We clasped hands for the lift, and a trace of fear flashed in Josh's eyes. It was the same look I'd seen over and over the past few days. I braced myself for another bailout, but then I felt the force of Josh's hands pressing on mine. He wasn't backing down!

He pushed me upward, and I locked my muscles into place, holding myself steady in the air. Excitement and joy bubbled inside me, but I suppressed all of it to make sure I held my position completely still. Josh rotated slowly as we moved across the ice, and I caught the huge smiles of Em and Sergei at the boards.

Josh lowered me into his arms, and he spun me around as we held on tight to each other, exhaling with laughter.

"That felt *so* good," I said.

He touched his forehead to mine. "Let's do it again."

And so we did. We knocked out the easy lifts and then did all the ones from our programs. Our movements were still tentative, but I was up in the air, and that was all that mattered.

At the end of the session we found Stephanie on the bleachers, and she gave us a genuine ovation. Josh hugged her, and her eyes watered again.

"Looks like my work here is done," she said.

"You headed to the airport soon?" Josh asked.

She nodded. "The car's waiting for me."

"Thank you again," I said. "I could say it a million times and it wouldn't be enough."

"Well, I didn't do it for entirely unselfish reasons. I got to skate with Josh again, which I thought would never happen."

Josh smiled. "It was like we hadn't missed a beat."

"Will you be able to come to Greensboro?" I asked.

"Nationals? I... umm..." Stephanie stammered in surprise. "I have school, so I'll have to check my schedule."

"We'd really like you to be there," Josh said.

Her mouth curved into a little smile. "I'll try to make it happen."

We walked her out to the lobby to say our goodbyes, and we watched through the glass doors as she climbed into the town car. I shook my head as I reflected on what a strange and unexpected morning it had been.

"What's wrong?" Josh asked.

"Oh... nothing. I was just thinking about how unpredictable life can be."

"Today it was finally unpredictable in a good way," Josh said.

I laughed. "Yes. We need more of these good surprises. We've had more than enough bad ones lately."

He grasped my hand and kissed the back of it. "2011 is going to be nothing but awesomeness. I can feel it."

"So, you see us doing very well at nationals?"

He grinned. "We are going to blow everyone away at nationals with our amazing comeback."

"Only if you get to work," Em said behind us.

We turned toward her, and she stood with her hands on her hips and a stern look on her face. Her serious expression cracked, and we all laughed together. We'd been so tense with worry lately at the rink that the feeling of lightness made me giddy.

Then I remembered just how much we had to get done in four weeks.

Chapter Eleven

I pulled my hair into a tight ponytail and checked my makeup in the locker room mirror. I didn't usually wear makeup for practice, but at nationals every little detail was scrutinized. The judges watched all the practices, which meant I had to make an effort on my appearance.

My phone chimed in my bag, and I quickly looked at the alert. Josh and I had received so many tweets and messages of support since we'd been in Greensboro. The latest was a best wishes post from a fan with a link to a local news feature on us. I clicked the "Like" button and made a mental note to watch the video later.

Walking down the corridor to the ice, I exchanged smiles and hellos with some of my competitors and their coaches. When I emerged from backstage, I stood at the boards and breathed in the smell of the freshly-cut ice. The large arena was almost empty and peacefully quiet since most fans hadn't arrived in Greensboro yet. A few days remained before the start of the senior-level events and most importantly, our short program.

I bounced on my skate guards and flexed my knees to

stay warm. Josh and I had practiced that morning at the much smaller rink adjacent to the Coliseum, and we'd done a solid run-through of our long program. We would normally rest and not utilize both practice sessions allotted for us, but we needed every moment on the ice we could get.

Em came up beside me with two cups of coffee, and I paused between bounces.

"Double fisting it already?" I said. "We're only on day four of the event."

She and Sergei had been in town longer for the novice and junior pair events, where our training mates had racked up a slew of medals. The younger generation of Team Cape Cod was the talk of the competition so far.

Em laughed and set the cups on the boards. "One of these is for Sergei. It does feel like we've been here more than four days, though."

The other teams in our practice group gathered around me, and I looked up at the digital time on the scoreboard. We only had a minute until the session would begin.

"Where's Josh?" I said.

Em started toward backstage, but Josh came out of the tunnel with a dazed look in his eyes and not a smile to be seen. The vibe he gave me was much different from the happy one he'd had earlier. What had happened between the time we'd warmed up off ice and now?

The announcer came over the PA system, and as she read the pairs in the group, Josh and I gave Em our guards and stepped onto the ice. We went through our individual warm-up routines, circling the ice multiple times, and then came together to start our crossovers.

"You okay?" I asked.

He nodded but still didn't speak. He just took my hand and quickened his step.

We made a few passes around the rink and warmed up our triple twist and our throw technique with an easy single.

Since we would be first in the group to have our music played, we went over to Em and Sergei at the boards for a drink of water and instructions for our short program run-through.

"Mark the jumps and skip the footwork, but do everything else," Sergei said.

"Yes, Sir." I saluted him, hoping to make Josh smile.

I got nothing.

We skated to the middle of the ice and waited for the announcer to call our names. The smattering of fans applauded, and I put my hand on Josh's chest for our opening pose. His T-shirt rose and fell against my palm more rapidly than normal, sending a wave of fear over me. Josh put his hand on my hip, but he didn't lock eyes with me to complete the pose. Instead he stared down at the ice.

The romantic piano music began, and we glided together slowly at first before picking up speed. We blew through the triple twist and skated through the spots for the side-by-side jumps and the throw flip as Sergei had directed. Josh's grip on my hand grew more intense with each stroke we took, and a sinking feeling invaded my stomach.

We curved with the corner of the rink and set up for the lasso lift, but Josh's hands were shaking too violently to even attempt it. He pulled away and skidded into the boards, and I hurried to his side.

"Do you need water?" I asked.

He shook his head and took deep, extended breaths. *Why is this happening again?* I wanted to ask him, but he wouldn't have been able to answer me. I didn't understand what had gone wrong. He hadn't had any episodes since Stephanie had worked with him.

Our music continued to play while we camped at the boards. When Josh had his breathing under control he stood tall and said, "I'm sorry."

"You know you don't have to apologize to me. I just want to know why it happened."

He pushed his fingers through his hair and gripped the short locks. "I saw the video of the accident."

Oh no. I'd only seen it once, and Josh hadn't watched it at all. His doctor had suggested he shouldn't.

"Where?" I asked.

"Someone sent us a link to a news story on us, and I wasn't thinking and clicked on it. The first thing they showed was the accident."

I cringed and rubbed his arm. "Let's go talk to Em and Sergei."

We cut across the ice, and Josh told Em and Sergei what he had seen. Em made him continue to drink water even after he insisted he was fine. The few spectators who had shown up were all watching us and not the pair doing their run-through behind us.

"I want you both to stay off social media the rest of the week," Sergei said.

I didn't give any joking salutes that time.

"Are you good to keep going, Josh?" Em asked.

He replied with a stiff nod.

"You have a lot of time left on the session, so why don't you do the Salchows and the throw and then take another stab at the lift," Em said.

We entered the traffic of the other three teams and moved leisurely around the rink to regain our feel for the ice. I had questions for Josh about how the video had reignited his fears, but those had to wait until we finished practice.

We took off on the Salchows, and Josh landed wildly with his leg flying out and his upper body pitching forward. More problems came on the throw flip. I was already thinking about the lift coming up, and I slipped off my landing edge, sprawling my limbs over the ice.

I caught up to Josh and internally berated myself. I had no business making mistakes. With Josh dealing with so many demons, I had to be one hundred percent on my game.

We sped up our crossovers to get ready for the lift, and we grabbed hands for the swinging entry. Josh swung me up, and I wanted to scream with glee, but he stopped the motion before I made it above his head. His arms collapsed, and I came down on his back. I held onto him, sliding down until my feet hit the ice.

"It felt like we had it," I said.

Josh scrubbed his palms on his black pants. "My feet didn't feel right."

Sweat trickled down his hairline, and he wiped his face on the sleeve of his T-shirt. The lift would have worked if Josh had kept going. I knew with absolute certainty there hadn't been a technique problem. It was all in Josh's head.

We didn't make any more attempts during the session, and the media was all over us in the mixed zone afterward. We tried to avoid directly answering the questions about the aborted lifts. No one knew the problems Josh had experienced, and we were going to keep them private. Our answers centered on how happy we were to be competing again. We had to spin any positives we could find.

After I changed out of my workout gear, I went out to the shuttle bus that would take us to the hotel. I expected to see Josh on the bus, but he wasn't there and he didn't show up before we pulled away from the arena. I found him at the hotel, already in our room, sitting on the bed with his head in his hands.

Moving beside him, I put my arms around him and rested my chin on his shoulder. "You've come so far since the accident. Don't let this set you back."

He slowly sat up. "I didn't think seeing the video would affect me so much, but as soon as I saw it, that feeling of dread came back... like I had no control over anything. And then when I walked into the arena, it reminded me of the last time we skated in a place like that, and I saw us falling all over again."

"You do have control. You've been in complete control on the ice since Christmas. When you start to doubt yourself, think about all the great practices we had at home."

He arched his neck back and let out a loud breath. "This is so frustrating. I never thought I'd have stage fright skating in a big arena."

"Maybe we can ask the organizers to move the pairs competition to the practice rink." I smiled a little.

His lips made a half-hearted attempt to return my gesture. I leaned over the side of the bed and reached into the outside pocket of my bag for the color-coded event schedule.

"We have practice at the secondary rink tomorrow, and then we have the twenty-minute warm-up Thursday morning at the arena. That'll give you a chance to get comfortable there, and we can work through any issues before the short that evening."

"We should be worrying about normal stuff like landing jumps and keeping our spins in sync instead of..." His voice tightened. "You're supposed to be able to count on me to be strong, and I'm a freaking mess."

My fingers clenched into a fist. I wanted to strangle the person who had sent the video. I knew no harm had been meant, but it had put Josh back in that dark place. I couldn't let him get swallowed up by it again.

"If you weren't strong, you wouldn't be here right now, about to compete two months after a terrifying injury. A lot of people wouldn't come back from that." I turned his face toward me. "I believe in you, and I believe in us."

He gazed at me a long minute. "I just want to be the partner you deserve. The man you deserve."

"You are. You are everything I need and so much more." I softly kissed him and whispered on his lips, "So much more."

He cradled my head between his hands and pressed his mouth to mine with more intensity. I felt how much he wanted to show me his strength and to conquer everything he was battling. I'd spoken from my heart when I'd said I believed in him, but I feared he needed more than sheer will to finally slay his demons.

****

The aroma of coffee surrounded me as I sat at a table in Café Expresso, waiting for Josh to join me. He'd let me use the bathroom mirror first to do my competition hair and makeup, so he was still getting ready. I'd been too jumpy sitting in the room and had gone downstairs to sit in the café and watch the lobby activity.

"Coco!" Quinn squealed and ran from the elevator bank into the open café. Liza trailed behind her.

"Hey, Cutie." I tickled Quinn's stomach.

She giggled and climbed onto the chair next to mine. "Mommy said I been a good girl all week, so Sissy gonna get me a treat."

"Where's Alex? Has he not been good?" I asked.

"No, he was a bad boy."

"He apparently had a meltdown at Fan Fest this morning," Liza said. "Something involving a teddy bear."

Quinn reached up to one of the braids in my up-do. "Your hair look so pretty."

"Be careful." I leaned away from her little fingers. "It took me half an hour to get these right."

"You usually do those in no time," Liza said.

"My hands were shaking too much."

Liza sat cross-legged on the chair across from me. "My dad said Josh didn't have a good warm-up this morning."

I fiddled with the ends of my jacket sleeves. Despite my pep talk a few days earlier, Josh had been a walking and skating bundle of nerves. It was like his self-doubt blockaded all the positivity I kept feeding him.

"He was so tight on everything, and we only got one lift in the air for two seconds before he bailed. I have no idea what's going to happen tonight."

Quinn wandered over to the dessert case, and the girl working the counter struck up a conversation with her. I looked longingly at the brownies, thinking how much I could use the chocolate comfort.

"I wish I could be there to cheer for you guys," Liza said.

"I know you'll be watching online while you get ready in your room," I said. She had her own short program to perform later that night. "How are you feeling?"

"I've been playing Barbie with Quinn so I don't keep running my program in my head."

"You're going to be awesome. You're so trained for this."

Josh walked up, rolling his bag, and he looked as tense as he had when I'd left our room.

"Hey, Liza. Ready to go, Court?"

Quinn heard his voice and abandoned the desserts for him. "Good luck, Josh."

His face relaxed a bit, and he ruffled Quinn's curls. I gathered my bags and gave both Liza and Quinn hugs.

"Go get 'em tonight." I gave Liza an extra squeeze.

"You, too."

Josh and I boarded the bus and rode in silence for the short trip to the arena. I wasn't going to keep asking if he was okay because I knew the answer. His knees hadn't stopped bouncing since we'd taken our seats.

Once we arrived at the arena, we each plugged in our iPods and set off on a light jog through the backstage corridors. My heart rate was more elevated than usual as we jogged and stretched the minutes away. The anxiety of not knowing how Josh would react come show time was burning a hole in my stomach.

Em and Sergei had arrived while we warmed up, and they stood along the wall, observing us. When Josh went to the locker room to store his iPod, Em pulled me aside.

"You hanging in okay?" she asked.

"Not really. I don't know what's going to happen out there. Josh was freaked out just from skating in the near-empty arena. How's he going to handle the crowd? He might have a panic attack in the middle of the program."

"We're going to do everything we can to put him at ease."

"He was doing so well, and then that stupid video jacked it all up." My voice rose with each word.

Em put her hands on both sides of my face. "You have to stay calm. Josh needs you to be steady and confident. He needs your positive energy."

I kept my eyes on her unblinking stare and slowed my breathing with a long inhale and exhale. Em was right. I had to get it together and help Josh through this.

He returned from the locker room, and we walked through our program on the floor, engaging in minimal conversation. Em and Sergei gave us constant encouragement and continued to do so after we donned our costumes. We worked our way to the edge of the ice for the six-minute warm-up, and I watched Josh's eyes pan over the crowd. His Adam's apple dipped slowly as he took a hard swallow.

Please don't freak out. Please don't freak out.

"Would the following couples please take the ice," the announcer boomed.

We heard our names and hopped onto the ice, surrounded by the audience's loud cheers. We quickly accelerated and let our matching strokes take us around the rink. Sergei had told us to practice the twist and our jumps first, so we dodged the other three teams to prepare for the twist. We completed it cleanly and moved on to the Salchows, where Josh tripped and stumbled through the landing.

My stomach flip-flopped, knowing the element we had to practice next. We stopped at the boards for sips of water, and

Josh's hand shook as he capped his bottle. Em cupped his shoulder.

"Just take your time. Focus on the technique and nothing else," she said.

He nodded, and we found an open space on the ice to set up for the lift. Josh's sweaty palms gripped mine, and I wasn't surprised when he released me a moment later. With the crowd buzzing and three other pairs whizzing around us, there was entirely too much chaos for him.

"Keep going," I said. "Let's do the death spiral."

We spent the final minutes of the warm-up checking off our other elements, and as the clock hit zero I took Josh's hands and made him face me. We were first in the group to skate, so I had only a few moments to try to get through to him.

"Do you remember what Stephanie said?" I looked firmly into his eyes. "This is home. The ice is *our* home."

I saw him processing that truth, and I squeezed his hands. "Nothing in the past matters. Only this moment and you and me. We are in total control."

He stared back at me, his blue eyes showing his fight to clear the doubt. He pulled me into his arms, holding me tight to his body, and we only parted when the announcer started our introduction. We took our place at center ice, and I prayed one last time we would get through the program without disaster.

The music began, and we glided along to the opening piano notes, skating into the triple twist without much speed. I spun three times as quickly as I could and dropped into Josh's fumbling catch. My pulse kicked into a higher gear as I worried the clumsy exit was a sign of things to come.

Our speed increased as we circled the rink in preparation for the side-by-side jumps. We pushed off from the ice, and I tried to watch Josh to see if he would land cleanly. With my focus on him, I slipped off my own landing edge and splatted onto the ice. Meanwhile, Josh had completed the Salchow perfectly.

Nice going, Court. Way to be steady and on your game.

I scrambled to my feet and met up with Josh. There was no time to dwell on the mistake because the throw triple flip loomed. Josh moved behind me and grasped my hips, and when I jabbed the ice with my toe pick, he sprang me into the air. I put all my focus on coming down on a clean edge, and I didn't botch the landing that time.

We curved into the straight-line footwork, and with the lift coming next, I channeled my nervous energy into achieving level-four steps. By the time we finished skating from one end of the rink to the other, my heart was pounding both from exhaustion and fear of what Josh was going to do. Or not do.

We came around the corner of the rink and joined hands for the lasso entry. I held my breath, anticipating all the possible outcomes, but praying for the best. Before I realized what was happening, Josh had swung me up over his head. I was airborne!

I exhaled and held on fiercely as he began to rotate, but I held my breath again when I changed positions, setting my hand on his shoulder. That had been the moment when the lift had gone terribly wrong at Skate America.

Josh's feet crawled across the ice, but he was moving! The audience's cheers were the loudest yet, and they grew to a roar when Josh gently set me down. They understood the importance of that element to us. Josh's eyes were wide but shining so brightly, and I broke into a huge smile.

The side-by-side spins and the death spiral were a blur as all I could think about was giving Josh the biggest hug I'd ever given him. We spun into our ending pose, and I threw my arms around him as if we had won the Olympics. He buried his face in my hair and shook with tears. That made my chest burst with emotion and set off a cascade of waterworks in my eyes.

I had never received a standing ovation for an imperfect performance, but the crowd was on its feet, acknowledging the tough road we had travelled. We bowed to every side of the arena and hugged each other again as we skated to the boards. Em and Sergei had wet eyes, too, and they embraced us and choked out, "So proud of you" over and over through their tears.

We sat in the kiss and cry to wait for our score, but I didn't care about the numbers. We could be in last place and I'd still feel victorious. I linked my arm through Josh's, and he laced our fingers together and leaned close to my ear.

"Thank you," he said.

I turned to face him. "For what?"

He rested his forehead on mine. "For giving me all your patience."

"I told you I'll always be by your side. No matter what."

He kissed the top of my head, and we looked up at the monitor as our score was announced. The numbers were respectable, and with only a few teams left to skate, we sat in sixth place.

"Sorry about the Sal," I said. "That was such a stupid mistake."

"Are you kidding? Don't even think of apologizing after all the angst I put you through."

Em and Sergei motioned for us to follow them backstage, and they hugged us again. Sergei kept his arm around me and patted my shoulder.

"Don't worry about the jump," he said. "We couldn't be happier with how you both skated. You showed so much courage today."

"I can't thank you guys enough." Josh looked between Em and Sergei. "You never got frustrated with me. Not even when I wanted to slap myself upside the head."

Em laughed and rubbed his back. "We always knew you

had the strength to rise above it. We just wanted to give you the support you needed."

Neither Josh nor I could stop smiling as we left them and met the media. When we finished in the mixed zone, we changed and headed upstairs to look for Stephanie, my parents, and Mrs. Cassar. Stephanie found us first.

"Thanks for scaring me to death in the warm-up." She punched Josh's arm but then hugged him. "I thought I was going to have to run onto the ice and talk you through it again."

"Court used some of your wise words to help me," Josh said.

Stephanie turned to me with raised eyebrows and an actual look of approval. I'd take any little bit of further progress between us.

"You know, you guys are only a few points out of fourth place. The rest of the competition was a disaster," she said. "You can still get a medal."

"You want us to win a medal?" Josh asked with grin.

"I'm in favor of anything that will irritate Mom. She's been so obnoxious lately."

I stifled a laugh. *Lately?*

"We'd love to be on the podium, but we just want to enjoy the long now that the pressure is off," Josh said.

"Definitely," I agreed. "At this point, a medal would just be a huge bonus."

"Well, if you could try to make it happen that would be fabulous." Stephanie put her hand on her chest. "I'd love nothing more than to go home and tell Mom I was pivotal in your success."

I laughed to myself again. Stephanie was probably going to take credit for every achievement we had from then on.

But, hey, it's much better than her spitting on our partnership.

While she and Josh chatted, I watched Josh laugh and smile, and a deep surge of happiness filled me. I couldn't wait to get back on the ice with him and skate our long program. We'd worked so long and so hard to have that moment, and we wouldn't have any more worries weighing us down. We could skate with our focus all on one thing — showing our love for each other.

Chapter Twelve

I looked up at Josh and pinched my hand to make sure I wasn't dreaming. I had skated our long program time and again in my head, yearning for the chance to perform it under the bright lights, in front of a cheering crowd. That moment had finally come.

We stood in the middle of the ice, me in a flowy, cream-colored dress and Josh in a matching shirt and beige pants. We looked like Lizzie and Mr. Darcy as we prepared to skate to music from the movie *Pride and Prejudice*. Josh wasn't brooding like Mr. Darcy, though. He was gazing at me with an abundance of love. The happiness I felt combined with all the competition adrenaline had my pulse going haywire.

On the second joyful note of the music, we began our equally joyful steps. The positive energy flowing through both of us led us to complete our difficult opening elements easily. Josh pressed me into the air for the star lift, and he turned smoothly over the ice. His confidence had returned to the level he'd had at home.

He set me down, and we slowed as the music transitioned to my favorite piece on the soundtrack. Josh had used our love story as his inspiration when choreographing the program, and the bubbly first section represented our blossoming friendship. The second section, set to the slow and romantic "Your Hands Are Cold," showed us falling in love.

Josh swept me into his arms, and we were so close our noses touched. His eyes dropped to my lips, and for a second I lost myself completely in him and the music. The passion burning between us overwhelmed me. I wanted nothing more than to bottle that moment because it was absolute perfection.

We had to break apart to move into our spirals, and some of my nervous energy resurfaced. Our double Axel sequence coming up was one of our iffiest elements. We skated side by side, each of us setting up for the jump's forward entry. On the same beat, we launched ourselves into the air and spun two-and-a-half times. As soon as we landed, we repeated the jump. Josh landed the second one slightly after I did, but I still fist pumped inside. We would have plenty of time to work on our unison for the future.

Josh took my hand, and we hit our lasso lift right on the crescendo of the music. My heart soared as high as my position in the air. I flew above the ice with deafening applause all around me, and I had only one thought — *Does the program have to end?*

We sailed through the rest of the elements, and we came together hand in hand, eyes locked on one another, for the final soft notes. Josh enveloped me in an embrace, and I rested my head on his chest as the music ended. The crowd roared with cheers, but we didn't move. I closed my eyes and pressed myself against him, soaking in his warmth and the surrounding mania we had inspired.

"I love you," Josh said.

I lifted my head and kissed his lips. "I love you, too."

I floated on a cloud through our bows, the kiss and cry, and the interviews backstage. We were in first place with the final group of four teams left to skate, so we had moved up at least one spot. We were headed upstairs when my phone rang, and I saw the caller was my former partner.

"Hey, Mark."

"Hey, congratulations. You guys were great."

I smiled at his enthusiasm. "Thanks. That means a lot to me."

"Watching you almost made me want to get back out there, and then I remembered triple run-throughs and I was happy to be on my couch."

I laughed. "I'm glad you're enjoying your retirement."

"I am. And I'm glad you're still enjoying skating. You and Josh really do look great together. You do those romantic programs much better than you and I did." He chuckled.

I spotted Mom coming toward Josh and me with her arms open for a hug, so I thanked Mark again for the call and dropped the phone into my bag. Both my parents and Mrs. Cassar showered us with congrats on the concourse while Stephanie kept a close eye on the competition. When the last pair took the ice, we carried our bags down the steps and sat with her in the top row.

"You're in third right now!" She shook Josh's arm. "You're guaranteed a medal!"

"Are you serious?" My eyes shot up to the video board. Finishing fourth and winning the pewter medal would be beyond awesome after all we had gone through.

"If this team messes up, you can move up to bronze," Stephanie said.

"Steph," Josh chided her.

"What? Where's your ambition?"

"We're not going to cheer for someone else to screw up," he said.

She rolled her eyes. "Always the Boy Scout."

Josh shook his head but grinned at me. If Stephanie was going to be evil, at least she was on our side. I was still getting used to that.

The pair on the ice, a team just up from juniors, began their program to *The Phantom of the Opera*, and Stephanie groaned.

"Ugh, I'm so over this music."

Josh covered his mouth, and I couldn't tell whether he was muffling a laugh or a comment for his sister. I put my attention back on the ice and watched the young team skate slowly through their elements. Their jumps, throws, and lifts were less difficult than what Josh and I had done, and they didn't fill the rink with their skating. Everything looked small in comparison to the other teams, which was understandable for a new senior pair. I chewed on my thumbnail, wondering if our score just might beat theirs.

As we waited for the final standings, Josh held both my hands between his, saving my thumbnail from more abuse. The numbers popped up on the big screen, and Josh pumped my hands. We'd finished third!

I grabbed him for a hug. "I can't believe we got bronze!"

"Two days ago I thought we might be last," he said.

"I told you that you could get third," Stephanie said. "You're a million times better than those scrubs that just skated."

Josh and I both sat open-mouthed, searching for the right response.

"Umm... thanks, I'm glad you think so," I said.

We had to wait until much later that night to get our medals, so we filled the hours with a family dinner celebration and losing our voices cheering for Liza as she won her first national title. Josh didn't receive so much as a text from his parents, and sadly I wasn't surprised. He didn't seem fazed, though, as he received more than enough love from my parents and Mrs. Cassar.

When we finally stood on the podium, I kissed my medal and beamed at Josh standing behind me. "It's crazy how the same result can cause such different feelings. Last year bronze meant heartache and devastation, and this year I'm so ridiculously happy with it. This is now my favorite medal I've ever won."

He smiled and wrapped one arm around me. "This day is my favorite everything."

I couldn't wait to see the photos of the ceremony because Josh and I must have had the biggest, cheesiest smiles in all of them. We raced around the ice for the victory lap and exited to let the ice dance medalists take the stage. Our friends and family were sitting in the front row, and I presented my bouquet of blue flowers to Mrs. Cassar.

"None of this would've been possible without you," I said. "I wish we could give you more."

She reached down and touched my cheek and then Josh's. "You gave me the greatest thrill today. Seeing you do all those hard tricks so beautifully and with so much passion for each other was the best gift you could give me."

Quinn scooted forward on Em's mom's lap. "I wanna see your medal."

I pulled the red, white, and blue ribbon from around my neck and handed it to her. She peered at it and ran her finger over the lettering.

"I gonna win one when I get older," she said.

She had just started taking lessons, but I had no trouble believing she would be a winner someday. With Em and Sergei's genes and her tenacity, she had the makings of a legendary superstar.

"No doubt you will, Miss Aquinnah," I said.

"You two are all the talk on social media," Stephanie said as she scrolled on her phone. "No one cares about the champions."

"Everyone loves a good comeback story," Mrs. Cassar said.

Mom leaned over the railing and patted Josh's shoulder. "You both must be exhausted after the week you've had."

"I actually feel better than I have in months," Josh said.

"Me, too. I'm ready to dance." I shimmied my hips.

"Are you going to the lame competitors' party?" Stephanie asked.

"Yes, we are." Josh hugged me to his side. "I've been waiting almost ten years to dance with this girl at the party."

I stood on the toes of my skate guards and pecked his cheek. "I'm all yours."

****

In the dark hotel ballroom, skaters of all ages busted out their best dance moves around us. A couple of novice kids almost crashed into me while doing The Dougie, and Josh shielded me with his body.

"It's getting dangerous." I laughed.

He locked me inside his arms. "You're safe in here."

I smiled and put my hands around his waist, and our hips moved together to the hip-hop rhythm. We'd been fused together on the dance floor since we'd arrived.

"You know, I remember seeing you at this party every year," I said. "You were always off to the side with your friends… never dancing."

"There was only one reason I came to the parties, and that was to watch you," he said, coiling one of my curls around his finger.

"I don't remember feeling like I was being watched."

"That's because I had the whole stealth admirer thing down cold."

He treated me to one of his little shy grins, and I brought my hands up to his face.

"The fact that you were still enamored with me after witnessing my spastic dancing tells me you're definitely a keeper," I said.

"You were so damn cute. I wanted to ask you to dance so

bad."

"You should have. I would've said yes in a hot second. You were pretty damn cute, too." I teased my fingers into his hair. "Still are."

His body tightened against mine, and he bit his bottom lip. "Now that I've fulfilled my fantasy of being here with you, why don't we continue the party in a more private place?"

I smiled. "Not so shy anymore, are you?"

We snaked through the crowd and entered the cool air of the lobby. As we passed one of the three bars in the hotel, Josh stopped and pointed inside.

"I need to get something real quick. I'll be right back."

I gave him a curious look, wondering what he would be getting in a bar. A few minutes later he came out, holding a bottle of champagne and two glasses.

"What's this?" I asked.

"Champagne."

"I know that, Silly, but what are *you* doing with it?"

"What better way to have my first drink than with celebratory champagne?" He grinned.

When we reached our room, I turned on the desk lamp and plugged my iPod into the alarm clock. I clicked on my R&B playlist and danced over to Josh while slipping off my ballet flats.

"Let the party continue," I said as he twirled me around.

He tore the paper from the top of the champagne bottle and aimed the cork away from us. With a loud pop, the cork went flying onto the bed and champagne spilled out.

"Whoa." Josh swung the bottle over the desk so it wouldn't drip onto the carpet. He filled our glasses and handed me one. "We have to do a toast, of course."

"Do you have one in mind?"

"I do." His eyes captured mine and lingered there. "I've wanted to say this to you since we skated this afternoon."

My heart beat a little faster, and I shifted closer to Josh.

He lifted his glass, never breaking his gaze on me.

"To my partner and my best friend." He paused. "I imagined this day so many times, skating with you at nationals, giving everything we have to each other, and it was beyond anything I could've ever imagined." He gently tucked my hair behind my ear. "*You* are beyond all my fantasies… and I've had some really great ones about you."

He gave me a devilish smile, and every part of my body filled with heat. I was about to knock the champagne from his hand so I could get to his delicious lips first.

"Thank you for making all my dreams come true," he said.

I melted inside from his words and from the way he was looking at me. His glass clinked against mine, and we took long sips. Josh hummed quietly in satisfaction.

"This is pretty tasty," he said.

"You're not going to become a lush on me?"

He laughed. "Nah, I'll save it for special occasions."

"Like when we win gold next year?" I smiled and ran my finger down his chest.

His face grew serious. "So you want to keep competing?"

My hand froze on his sweater. "Of course. Don't you?"

"Yes, definitely. I just wasn't sure how you felt since this season has been so rough. I didn't know if you wanted to take the chance of more crazy things happening."

I exhaled with relief. "All the injuries and setbacks in the world couldn't stop me from skating with you. Even with the craziness, I still loved every single second of being your partner. Do you know how excited I get each morning knowing I'm going to skate with you?"

"If it's as excited as I get every time I'm with you on *and* off the ice, I have a good idea." His thumb brushed lightly across my cheek.

I leaned into his touch and raised my glass. "Then to our beautiful partnership."

We tapped our glasses together and emptied them, and Josh lifted my chin. His lips caressed mine, giving me a much better buzz than the alcohol.

"Do you want more champagne?" I murmured.

He didn't answer, but he took my glass and set it on the desk with his. He curled one hand around my hip and the other behind my neck. The fire in his eyes stole my breath.

"I want *you*," he said.

He kissed me, and I wrapped my arms around him, joining us together and sealing the end of the perfect day.

Chapter Thirteen

Six Weeks Later

"What a gorgeous night." I tilted my head back to gaze at the sky full of twinkling light. "There must be a million stars out."

Josh unlocked his front door and took my hand. "I ordered them especially for your birthday."

I smiled and followed him inside. "Thank you for the romantic candlelight dinner. I've always wanted to eat at the Chatham Bars Inn."

We shed our coats and tossed them over the kitchen chairs, and Josh grasped both my hands, leading me to the sofa.

"The dinner wasn't your only gift." He sat me on the couch while he remained standing in front of me. "I have a surprise for you."

He unknotted his tie and slipped it from under his dress shirt collar, and I lifted my eyebrows. "Are you going to give me a show?"

His mouth stretched into a slow grin. "That'll come later."

He bent over me and placed the tie over my eyes, knotting it behind my head. His fingers combed through my hair and under my chin, and I shivered from anticipation.

"I don't trust you not to peek," he said, his breath tickling my lips.

"Curiosity is killing me."

He eased me back against the cushions. "Sit back and relax. The wait is almost over."

His warmth left me, and I listened hard for any clues of his surprise. He was so quiet I wondered if he had left the room. Finally, I heard some rustling, and a few moments later, a sound that was music to my ears both literally and figuratively.

The piano.

I gasped and ripped off the blindfold. Josh sat at his keyboard, playing "Exogenesis Symphony Part 3." I couldn't take my eyes off his beautiful hands dancing over the keys. I'd missed that sight *so* much. Tears tightened my throat, and I smiled as I noticed Josh had rolled up his sleeves to show off the bracelet I'd given him. It looked as amazing in action as I'd thought it would.

Josh wore a look of such peace as he played that my tears of joy couldn't be contained. I wiped them from my face and went to stand beside the keyboard as Josh finished the final stanza.

He hit the last note and looked up at me with a brilliant smile. I dropped onto the bench and threw my arms around him.

"When did this happen?" I cried.

"The last couple of weeks it all started to get easier. Every time I heard a song on the radio, I could picture myself playing it. I used the sheet music first, and then I was able to play them from memory — all my favorite songs."

His eyes shone as brilliantly as his smile, and I placed enthusiastic kisses all over his face and his mouth.

"I was going to tell you, but I thought I'd surprise you for your birthday," he said.

"Best. Gift. Ever."

I hugged him again, and he held me closer, pressing his cheek to my hair.

"There were some days…" he said quietly. "I was afraid I'd never remember."

I rubbed my hand along his back. "I'm so, *so* happy for you."

He slowly pulled his head back to face me. "Would you like to hear 'Over the Rainbow?'"

"I would love that."

As he began my favorite rendition, I rested my head on his shoulder. I loved being so close to him while he played and feeling the joy that always radiated from him.

When he finished I kissed his cheek, and he rattled off a string of impromptu cheerful notes, making us both laugh.

"Having that autographed sheet music up there was great inspiration." He pointed to his framed gift on the wall. "I've been thinking a lot about the song and how it would make an awesome long program."

"Totally. We should get with Em and Sergei on it right away."

"I was thinking we could save it… for the Olympic season."

"Oh." I shifted my eyes to the keyboard.

"I know we said we'd take it one year at a time, but I couldn't help but think ahead. If you don't want to keep skating until 2014, though, I understand. It's a lot to deal with and—"

"No, it's not that. I haven't ruled anything out yet. I just… I don't want to look that far ahead. I did that with Mark — focused too much on the Olympics — and I don't want to get wrapped up in that again. I want to focus on living in the moment and enjoying every day of skating with you."

He smiled and put his arm around me. "That sounds like a great plan."

"This is why we make such an awesome team." I patted his thigh.

"Except… I do still want to save the Muse song… for a season that shall remain nameless."

I laughed and nodded. "I can agree to that."

I let my mind wander to that nameless season for a minute. It couldn't possibly be more difficult that what we had endured the past season. But then I remembered the pain and anguish I'd gone through twice trying to make the Olympic team, and my stomach twisted at the thought of experiencing that again.

Josh kissed my forehead as if he knew exactly what I needed at that moment. With him by my side, I had to believe things would be different because there was one thing I knew with absolute certainty — I was wholeheartedly his, and he was undeniably mine, and there was nothing stronger than the love between us.

More Books by Jennifer Comeaux

To stay up to date on Jennifer's new releases, join her mailing
list:
http://eepurl.com/UZjMP

Edge Series
Life on the Edge (Edge #1)
Edge of the Past (Edge #2)
Fighting for the Edge (Edge #3)

Ice Series
Crossing the Ice (Ice #1)

Coming Soon
Taking the Ice (Ice #3)

Jennifer loves to hear from readers! Visit her online at:
jennifercomeaux.blogspot.com
www.twitter.com/LadyWave4
jcomeaux4@gmail.com

Please consider taking a moment to leave a review at the
applicable retailer. It is much appreciated!

About the Author

Jennifer Comeaux is a tax accountant by day, writer by night. There aren't any ice rinks near her home in south Louisiana, but she's a diehard figure skating fan and loves to write stories of romance set in the world of competitive skating. One of her favorite pastimes is travelling to competitions, where she can experience all the glitz and drama that inspire her writing.

Acknowledgements

My first thank you goes to the readers! Thank you for sharing your love of Courtney and Josh's story with me and for always inspiring me to write more. I can't tell you how much your messages mean to me!

I owe a huge thanks to my beta readers Teresa, Sylvianne, Debbie, and Christy. It helps so much to have you along on my journey with each book! Christy, thank you for helping me devise the plot for this book. I was banging my head against a brick wall, and our plotting sessions made all the difference! I also owe thanks to Christy, Marni, and Melissa for proofreading. Every minute of your time you've given me is much appreciated!

9 780990 434221